The Perfect Gift

Bluegrass Single #3

Kathleen Brooks

Prologue

The small island country of Rahmi, seventeen years ago . . .

N abi Ulmalhamash Mosteghanemi stood motionless in front of his father and King Ali Rahman. His hands were clasped behind his back and his short, slightly wavy black hair was slicked back from his face. His father stared emotionlessly at him while the king congratulated him on his twenty-first birthday.

For twenty-one years, Nabi Ulmalhamash Mosteghanemi had been groomed by his father, the head of intelligence for the king. The trouble was he wasn't anything like his father. His father was imposing, strong, and fearless. He was the best decoder, the best tracker, and the best intelligence gatherer. Nabi was five-foot-eight inches tall and weighed one hundred twenty pounds. What he lacked in physical stature, he made up for in brains. He could hack a computer system faster than his father. As his mother liked to tell him, he held promise.

Upon graduating from the military academy in the summer, he was determined not to let any physical inequities hinder him from becoming the best soldier in all of Rahmi. At school, he'd focused on his studies and took hope from his idol, Ahmed Mueez. Ahmed hadn't been very well known before he left Rahmi at the age of eighteen. But now he was perhaps the most notorious living legend in the world. He made black market dealers shake in their boots. He made foreign governments surrender before they were even attacked. He was simply the coolest badass on the planet, and Nabi was determined to be just like him.

"As a favor to your father, I have reviewed your records from the academy," King Ali Rahman said, drawing Nabi's attention. This was it. This was when he was going to be assigned to the king's personal staff just as his father had planned.

"While your test scores are the highest in your class, your physical scores are mediocre at best. I know you and your father were hoping for a palace position, but I do not believe you are ready."

Nabi didn't move as his heart plummeted. He saw the look of disappointment on his father's face and wanted to run from the palace in shame. But he did not. He stared straight ahead and refused to react to the news.

"As you know, one of our best soldiers was just like you. That is why I am sending you to Prince Mohtadi's farm in the United States." Nabi held his breath. Ahmed was there—his idol. "You will train with Ahmed until he has deemed you ready to become a member of the palace guard with your father. You leave tomorrow. Happy birthday, Nabi Ulmalhamash Mosteghanemi."

The king gave a slight bow of his head to indicate he was finished, and Nabi bowed quickly before walking calmly from the chambers. The thick, ornately carved doors closed behind him as he punched the air with his fist and excitedly whispered, "Yes!"

Nabi hurried through the gardens and out the main entrance of the palace. He jogged down the road to a row of houses reserved for palace staff. His mother would be making his birthday cake right about now. He ran up the path and pushed open the door.

"Mother! I just got the best birthday gift!" Nabi hurried into the kitchen where his mother was icing his favorite cake. "I'm going to the United States to train under Ahmed!" Nabi grabbed her up in a hug and lifted her off the ground. He saw his mother's eyes tear at the thought of him leaving. "Don't worry, Mother."

She reached up and patted his cheek. "I'm not worried. I'll just miss my boy. You'd better start packing. Remember, Nabi Ulmalhamash Mosteghanemi, you need to be strong and serious. Don't let anyone push you around."

"Yes, Mother!" Nabi called as he raced to pack.

Nabi stood in front of the double doors leading to the hospital's labor and delivery wing and cringed. He'd been in Keeneston, Kentucky, for several months, and he still didn't know what to think. It was as if he were living in an alternate universe. Keeneston was a small town outside of Lexington. Most of the residents worked for the town, owned farms, or had shops on Main Street.

He was working and learning from his idol, but nothing else was going according to plan. The more he tried to be in charge and the more serious he acted, the more people rolled their eyes at him and said something he didn't understand, like "Bless your heart." But the prince and princess were the worst. They insisted he call them Mo and Dani. Twenty-one years of training had taught him to bow in their presence, yet *Dani* would get mad at him for doing so.

Nabi looked back through the doors as he heard a scream coming from Her Royal Highness. She was about to give birth to a royal heir of Rahmi. He was charged with protecting the door, although he didn't know from whom. No one in this strange town seemed to care about members of the royal family living among them. They were treated like everyone else. No one bowed; no one called them by their titles . . . he was absolutely baffled.

The only good thing was that Ahmed's training had put twenty pounds on Nabi. He had also begun a late growth spurt. Ahmed said the same happened to him when he was in his early twenties. Nabi puffed up with pride as he stood against the doors. He was going to be a strong soldier like Ahmed. He was off to a good start; after all, he was guarding the royal heir!

The sound of running feet caught his attention. He leaned forward to determine if they were running toward or away from the doors he was guarding. *Toward, definitely toward.* Nabi put his hand on the gun he had hidden underneath his black suit jacket but relaxed when he saw it was only four old women who ran toward him.

"Get out of the way, Nabi!" Miss Daisy Mae Rose ordered.

He narrowed his eyes. No one called him by his full name here.

Miss Lily Rae Rose slid to a stop in her orthopedic shoes. "Come on, you heard my sister. Scoot!"

"Yeah, we have a new citizen of Keeneston to welcome," Violet Fae Rose, the third of the Rose sisters, said with her hands on her generous hips.

"I have the gift basket," Edna, Miss Lily's neighbor, huffed as she lifted up a basket filled with homemade goodies.

Nabi held up his hands. "I am sorry. I cannot let anyone through."

4

"Hmph. Well, bless your heart, I know you're just trying to do your job, but you need to move." Miss Lily and her white-haired horde pushed forward.

Nabi took a step backward. His heels pushed up against the door as he heard the sound of more feet running toward them. John Wolfe — the town's king of gossip — Kenna Mason Ashton and her new husband Will, and Will's mother, Betsy Ashton, hurried up to join the others.

"Move, Nabi," Kenna ordered.

"I cannot."

"Bless your heart, you will. You just don't know it yet," she said sweetly. Someone was going to have to explain to him what this saying meant.

"Are we too late?" Paige Davies Parker asked as she approached with her mother, Marcy Davies, and her sisters-in-law: Katelyn, Annie, Morgan, and Tammy.

Nabi felt himself being pushed backward. The handle of the door dug into his back as he held on for dear life. No training could prepare him for this. The mob was armed with cakes, casseroles, and baby booties. They were relentless as he locked his hands on the bar of the door and prayed he'd live to make it home. He was going to ask for a transfer tomorrow. Anything to get out of this crazy town!

Chapter One

Nabi woke with a start. Someone was in his room. Over the seventeen years he had lived on Mo and Dani's farm as their head of security, he had been woken up numerous times by people sneaking in. At first he thought it was strange, but now he was used to it.

He had locked his doors and windows, installed security, activated motion detectors . . . but that hadn't stopped her. It had barely slowed her down. And now he could tell by the breathing she was the one slowly creeping toward his bed in his small house on the farm.

He listened closely—five intruders in total. He kept his breathing normal and waited until exactly the right moment to attack. It might be dangerous letting them get this close, but Ahmed had trained him well. One, two, three . . .

"Argh!" Nabi yelled as he leapt from his bed with his arms outstretched. Ahmed had been right about the growth spurt. By the time Nabi was twenty-three, he stood just shy of six feet and was one hundred eighty-five pounds of pure muscle. He used every inch and every pound to his advantage as he tackled the intruders.

He took three of them down to the ground at once. As he looked up, he spotted his fourth target. He reached behind the curtain and pulled the intruder into his arms.

But where was their leader? Nabi scanned the room as he held the four prisoners against him. He listened, but not a sound was made. He felt it, but it was too late for him to stop it. Arms shot out from under the bed. They grabbed his ankles and yanked. He and the four trapped intruders fell in a heap to the ground. Or more accurately, he fell to the ground with the four intruders landing on top of him.

A slightly tanned face with blue eyes and dark brown, almost black, hair looked down at him as she stood up from under the bed.

"Happy birthday, Uncle Nabi!" Fifteen-year-old Abigail Mueez smiled before reaching back under the bed for the birthday cake she had hidden there. Her eleven-year-old brother, Kale, scrambled up from where he sat on Nabi's stomach. His mentor, Ahmed, and wife, Bridget, had kids that made breaking and entering look like an art form.

"I thought you men would be too old for this," Nabi grunted as Mo and Dani's nineteen-year-old twin boys, Zain and Gabriel, stood up.

"We're never too old to try to scare you, Uncle Nabi," Zain, the older twin, said.

"Besides, Ariana is only twelve. We have more tricks to show her," Gabe teased.

Mo and Dani's little girl, well, not so little anymore, flung her arms around his neck. "Happy birthday!" she said before kissing his cheek. She was quieter than her rambunctious older brothers. She had inherited her mother's shocking blue eyes and interesting shade of dark auburn hair. Her maternal grandmother was blond and it seemed to have mixed with Mo's dark hair. The result was stunning.

"Blow out your candle and make a wish." Abigail grinned as she lit the candle and held out the cake.

Thirty-eight years old. Nabi closed his eyes and blew out the candle. For seventeen years, he'd watched as people he originally thought were crazy turned into friends, got married, and had children. Everyone except him. He was the last man standing, and he hated it. He'd even seen kids who were just teenagers when he moved to town get married. He was close to asking his father to arrange a marriage just so he wouldn't be alone anymore. In fact, he had the email drafted, and all he had to do was hit Send.

Alone wasn't the right word. He was Uncle Nabi. He was the one the kids all gravitated to because they knew he wouldn't tell their parents what they told him. He knew about every party, every boy Abigail wanted to date, when Zain and Gabe had snuck out to meet girls. It made him feel old. No matter how much he loved teaching Kale how to hack a government computer system or sneaking Ariana out of boring social functions, he wanted his own child to hold, his own child to love.

"What did you wish for?" Ariana asked.

Nabi wrapped her in his arms and tossed her onto the bed as she giggled. Zain and Gabe did that weird twin thing where they didn't need to say a word yet had a whole conversation and were soon up on the bed jumping as Ariana got bounced around.

"You know I can't tell you, or it won't come true. I told my computer, though. I hope he doesn't spill the secret," Nabi teased as he slid a T-shirt on.

"Hurry up and get your shoes. Mom, Dad, Mo, and Dani have breakfast waiting at the main house," Kale told him as he pulled at Nabi's arm.

"I'm coming. Let me just send my birthday wish off, and then I'll be there."

"You can do that later," Zain groaned. "I'm hungry!"

"Me, too. We're growing boys after all," Gabe teased. And they were. Both were over six feet tall already and were causing Mo and Dani's chef heart palpitations with the amount of food they ate.

"Maybe we got your birthday wish," Ariana said quietly.

"Fine." Nabi gave in as he slid on a pair of running shoes. Today was his day off, and he found athletic shorts and a T-shirt to be his favorite off-duty attire.

Nabi let Ariana and Kale each take a hand and drag him from the house. It was only a quarter mile to the main house. The kids ran with him, each singing different variations of "Happy Birthday."

As they approached the main house, he saw Ahmed and Bridget walking hand in hand. Bridget still looked lovely with her strawberry blond hair pulled back into a ponytail—and still very deadly. Nabi had never forgotten what Bridget did to save Ahmed from his archenemy all those years ago. His mentor waved, but Bridget just shook her head at the sight of him being led around by five kids.

"Happy birthday, Nabi!" Bridget called out. He was surprised she didn't have one of the police dogs with her. Her kennel was an elite training base for police and military dogs. It had grown over the years, and now they employed an entire specialized staff to care for and train the dogs in everything from bomb detection, to drug detection, to cell phone detection.

"Thank you," Nabi laughed as Kale jumped on his back, and he raced the rest of the way to the house.

"I assume Abigail beat your new alarm system?" Ahmed asked proudly as they walked up the front stairs.

"She sure did. Then put me on the ground. I can't believe she's only fifteen," Nabi said as he shook his head.

He was feeling old again.

The butler opened the door to the mansion, and Dani and Mo hurried to meet them in the entranceway. Mo was in a suit, even this early in the morning. He knew Dani was still desperately trying to convince him, after almost twenty years of marriage, that jeans were acceptable to wear on a horse farm. Nabi understood, though. It was hard to grow accustomed to a new way of life after the strict upbringing they all had in Rahmi. And Mo was still a prince even if Dani was a paralegal and an active outdoorswoman. However, since Zain and Gabe were in college at Yale, and Ariana was old enough not to need or want her parents around all the time, they had started attending more political functions on behalf of Mo's brother, King Dirar.

"Happy birthday!" Mo said as he shook his hand.

Dani kissed his cheek. "We have your favorite: biscuits and sausage gravy."

"Did the cook make it?" Nabi asked hesitantly.

"No," Dani grinned. "Miss Violet brought it over just a little while ago. And Miss Daisy brought you some fresh-baked cookies. Miss Lily brought you some banana nut bread. It's all in the dining room."

Nabi rubbed his hands together. After seventeen years, Mo still couldn't get his French cook to make any of the Blossom Café's best Southern cooking. At least the Rose sisters didn't mind making it for him, bless their hearts. He had surprised his parents when they last came to visit by sharing his favorite foods and even accidently said "y'all." What could he say? He had fallen in love with Keeneston and, as he took a bite of his breakfast, it was no secret why.

Chapter Two

Abigail Mueez, or Abby as everyone called her, looked down the table at Uncle Nabi. Something was up with him. He had a smile on his face, but he seemed distant. She knew he wasn't really her uncle, but he was closer to the kids who ran around Desert Sun Farm than any of their real uncles. Abby was of a mind to see him happy.

"Psst, Zain," she whispered across the table to her childhood playmate. Zain and Gabe were now young men, but she'd been playing with them since she was old enough to pick a lock. If she needed a co-conspirator, the twins were it.

"What?" Zain mumbled over huge bites of biscuits and sausage gravy.

"Did you think Nabi is acting a little differently?"

"Yes," Gabe answered for his twin.

"He said something about a wish list on his computer. I'm going to check it out. Maybe if we get him something from it, he'll cheer up."

"Dad's taking him out riding with Ahmed after breakfast. We could go then," Zain told her as he reached for another biscuit.

"I want to go with you," Ariana whispered.

"I do, too!" Kale told them excitedly before Abby could tell him to hush.

Too late. Abby saw her father's head turn their way. He raised an eyebrow in silent question. Abby raised one back at him and kept eye contact. Her father could intimidate everyone else in the world, but it didn't work on her or her mother. With a look that told her to stay in line, her father turned back to talking with the rest of the adults.

Abby tried not to roll her eyes at Ariana and Kale. They were just eight months apart and inseparable. "Fine, but you two will be the lookouts."

Abby waited until her mother went to check on the dog training center and Aunt Dani went to placate their chef before grabbing her brother and friends to sneak out the back door. She held up her hand, signaling them to stop as she saw her father, Nabi, and Mo ride past them. "Okay, all clear!"

"Gosh, I've missed Kentucky," Zain said as he and his brother flanked Abby. Kale and Ariana were running ahead of them, laughing about who knew what.

"I can't wait to go to college. Dad still won't let me date. To have the freedom to go where I want and do what I want," Abby sighed, "would be heaven."

"For you maybe," Gabe said sadly.

"For us it's a lot of hard work because studying is the only thing we can do without pretense," Zain told her.

"Everyone wants to be our friends because we're princes. We are constantly worried about dating because no one seems sincere. If our date isn't wonderful, then it could end up on the gossip sites," Gabe continued.

Abby scrunched up her nose. "That sucks."

"Yep. Keeneston is the only place we can be ourselves. I'm just glad we can spend this summer break here instead of going to Rahmi," Zain said with a smile on his face. Abby didn't know when, but sometime since they left they had become men. Handsome men, but ick, they were like brothers to her, and it grossed her out just admitting they were good-looking.

"Well, it's nice to have you here. I'm glad those prince lessons are done. Maybe you can help me run interference with Dad. We can say we're going out to the movies, and I can actually go out with Corey."

"Corey?" The twins both groaned at the same time.

"Sorry, Abs, but I agree with your dad on this one. That guy is a total tool." Zain made a face, and Gabe laughed.

"That's not fair! I didn't say anything when you lost your V card to . . ."

"No need to remind me," Gabe said has he held up his hands. "But, you're like our sister. We have to look out for you. And Corey . . . well, Corey's a player."

"Ugh!" Abby rolled her eyes. Growing up was no fun. Now her best friends were acting like her father. Did that suddenly happen when you turned eighteen?

Zain stretched forward and opened the door for her. "Ari, you and Kale keep lookout," he instructed before the three of them headed upstairs to Nabi's room.

"Should we feel bad for snooping?" Gabe asked as Abby opened the laptop.

"We're only snooping to make Nabi happy, so no. Besides, it didn't stop you all from reading my diary when you were younger."

The computer turned on, and she stared at the login. She tried a couple times and cursed under her breath. "I need Kale to open it."

Gabe went to the window and signaled for Abby's computer-genius brother. Kale stormed up the stairs with the subtlety of a hundred elephants. She rolled her eyes in the silent suffering of an older sister. If Kale didn't look so much like her dad, she'd swear he was adopted.

"Can you get through his password?" Abby asked as she handed him the laptop.

"No problem-o," Kale said as he started typing. Yep, he had to be adopted. "Here you go," Kale said twenty seconds later.

"Wow. Good job," Abby said as a draft email came onto the screen.

Zain and Gabe leaned forward, and they all sat motionless as they read the email to Nabi's father.

I have given up hope of finding a woman to love. Please arrange a marriage for me.

"An arranged marriage?" Abby gasped.

Zain shrugged. "It's still done in Rahmi among the upper class. Our father was the first prince to not have an arranged marriage."

"But look at how happy your parents are. Don't you want Nabi to have that?" Abby asked as her heart sank. She had no idea he was so sad.

"What can we do about it?" Gabe asked almost apologetically.

Abby slammed her hand on his desk. "We can find the perfect woman to love him!"

"You want us to play matchmaker?" Kale raised his lip in distaste.

"Yes. And we will need some help," Abby grinned as she pulled out her cell phone.

An hour later, the quiet of the empty driveway of the white

Victorian bed and breakfast disappeared as one vehicle after another pulled in and passengers got out. Doors slammed and greetings were made as members of the large, young group of friends and family started gathering on the quaint street full of old houses, large yards, and colorful flowers. Zain, Gabe, Abby, Kale, and Ariana hopped out as Ryan Parker pulled in right behind them. Ryan's younger brother, Jackson, and sister, Greer, followed him out of his truck.

Cade and Annie's children—Sophie, Colton, and Landon—quickly followed. Both sets of Cy and Gemma's twins were the next to join them. Reagan and Riley shot daggers at their younger twin brothers, Porter and Parker.

"I can't believe you spied on me!" Reagan yelled as she gave her younger brothers a shove.

"What? You were the one kissing that boy right on the doorstep," Porter shot back. "You're just lucky Dad didn't see you."

"It was only natural to cool you off," Parker grinned.

"By dumping a bucket of water on her?" Riley shot back. "Before we leave for college in the fall, I vow we will make your summer a living hell."

Pierce and Tammy's four children—Piper, Dylan, Jace, and Cassidy—joined the rest of the group a moment before Sienna and Carter made their way forward. Ryan, who had a long-standing crush on Sienna, much to her father's chagrin and her mother's amusement, ran a hand over his hair and looked around. As soon as he spotted Sienna, he sauntered over to her.

"Man, give it a rest," Carter, Sienna's eighteen-year-old brother, groaned as Ryan stopped to hug Sienna.

Sienna blushed. "It's good to see you. It's strange being back in town and working while you're off at college."

"You're so lucky you graduated this year. But, I have just one more year to go," Ryan said with pride.

"And then what?" Sienna asked.

Ryan shrugged. "I haven't worked that out yet. I'm thinking of the FBI or DEA. I'm actually leaving in two weeks for a summer internship at their headquarters in DC. I'm spending one month with the FBI and then one with the DEA. I'm hoping it will give me some idea of which field I want to go into."

"Wow," Sienna said, impressed. "That's so, grown-up. I guess I'll always think of you as a little kid." Sienna laughed as she waved at Marshall and Katelyn's daughter, Sydney, and her seventeen-year-old brother, Wyatt.

"Hi y'all," Wyatt called out as he joined the group forming in the driveway.

"We're all real sorry about your great-grandfather," Abby said as she gave him a hug before giving one to Sydney.

"Thank you. Great-Grandma Wyatt is taking it pretty well. She's just too stubborn to allow herself to grieve," Sydney told them before they were all wrapped up in hugs from the group. Beauford Wyatt had passed away two months before. The entire town of Keeneston and even some old Atlanta society had come to the funeral.

"Who are we missing?" Sienna asked as she started looking around the group.

"Layne, as usual," Piper sighed.

The black Mercedes Layne had received earlier that year for her eighteenth birthday from her parents, Miles and Morgan, tore down the street and, with a controlled slide, turned into the parking lot, barely missing one of Miss Lily's rose bushes.

"Sorry I'm late, y'all. I was volunteering with veterans

today," Layne called out as she hurried from the car while tying her long black hair into a sloppy bun. "What did I miss?"

"Nothing yet. Abby was waiting for everyone to get here before telling us what's going on," Sophie told her.

"Well," Abigail said once she had everyone's attention, "now that everyone is here, we need some real help."

Chapter Three

A bby led the large group up the sidewalk to the front of Miss Lily's bed and breakfast. Miss Lily and her sisters sat on the porch as they sipped sweet tea and waited for hugs from all the kids.

Finally, after what seemed like forever, Cassidy was on the swing with Miss Daisy and Miss Violet. The older boys leaned against the house and the older girls sat on the steps. Everyone else sat cross-legged on the wooden floor. Tea had been passed out, and everyone was quiet as they munched on Miss Violet's cookies.

"So, dear, care to share with us what was so important that we had to miss our crocheting group?" Miss Daisy asked.

"I think the better question, Daisy Mae, is whether we are the first to know it or if John already has the details." Miss Lily looked pointedly at Abigail and waited. Miss Lily and her gentleman caller, John Wolfe, were in a competition for gossip. John had an uncanny way of finding gossip — the prevailing theory was aliens were telling him. So, if Miss Lily could get a scoop, she'd cherish every second of it. And brag continually for a week.

"You're the first. It's about Nabi," Abigail started. "As you know, today is his birthday, and we wanted to get him the perfect gift. He told us about his wish being on his computer, so we snuck in and looked."

"Abigail, that wasn't nice of you," Sienna chided. At twenty-one, Sienna Ashton was the oldest and took that role seriously.

"Oh stuff it, Sienna," Abby shot back. "It was all done with good intentions. Remember, back when you were just eighteen, Nabi's the one who drove to Lexington and picked you up when you had too much to drink at that party, and he didn't tell your parents." Will and Kenna Ashton were very understanding parents under most circumstances. This would not have been one of those times.

Sienna shot her the *I'm the adult here* glare and then rolled her eyes. "Fine, we all love Nabi. What crazy expensive thing does he want? I assume that's why you need all of us."

Abigail let out a long breath. "He needs a wife."

"Darn tootin'," Miss Lily chimed in.

"We need to clear the betting books," Miss Daisy told them.

"He's our longest outstanding bet," Miss Violet clarified. The Rose sisters ran a betting ring on local tidbits: when someone would get married, when they'd have a child, if an upcoming baby would be a boy or girl, and other similar topics.

"No, I mean we have to find him one right now, meaning today! He's ready to email his father to arrange a marriage for him."

The kids gasped and started talking among themselves as Miss Violet explained what an arranged marriage was to Cassidy.

"But, Uncle Nabi should be in love with the person he marries. Just like in the movies or with Mommy and

22

Daddy," Cassidy said with all the outrage a nine-year-old could have.

"Exactly!" Abby called out. "We need to find his true love. She's here in Keeneston. We just have to find her."

"What about the lady who teaches yoga?" Ryan suggested. "She's hot enough, and flexible." He winked to his seventeen-year-old brother, Jackson, who just rolled his silver eyes that made Abby forget why they were there for a minute. She could get lost in those eyes.

"Tiffany Sanders is the new president of the Keeneston Belles. She's pretty nice," Sienna suggested.

"She is," twenty-year-old Sophie agreed. The Keeneston Belles were the up-and-coming elite of Keeneston society whose purpose was officially charitable, but really they were just looking to marry well. Once they married, they joined the prestigious Keeneston Ladies Group, which secretly ran the town. Their poor husbands just didn't know it, bless their hearts.

"But she's twenty-three years old," Piper pointed out. "That's like Sienna marrying him."

"Ew," Sienna said as she wrinkled her nose. "He's like, old."

"He's only thirty-eight, dear. But I agree that any of the Belles are just too young for our Nabi," Miss Lily said as she poured another glass of sweet tea.

"What about Geri Wright? She works on Dad's farm and she's thirty-six," Carter, who was just as horse crazy as his dad, Will Ashton, suggested.

Reagan and Riley, Cy and Gemma's eighteen-year-old twin girls, shook their heads. "She's been divorced five times already."

"He needs someone to take care of him some. He's always taking care of us," Wyatt said as they all nodded.

"And someone who likes kids," Greer, Paige and Cole's twelve-year-old added.

"And who is really, really old. Like thirty," twelve-year-old Colton told them.

"She needs to be nice," Landon, Cade and Annie's youngest son, said on the heels of his brother, Colton.

"She needs to be athletic," Zain said.

"In a fun outdoors way," Gabe finished. "Nabi loves horse riding, ATV racing, and stuff like that."

"But she also needs to be strong," Layne suggested. "Nabi sometimes has to leave and can't tell us where he's going. She needs to be secure enough to handle that."

Abby agreed. And if anyone could see that, it was Layne. She had a serious business side from her mother, Morgan, and her father, Miles, who was a former Special Forces soldier. Layne could take out a man three times her size, while maintaining a pretty appearance with her black hair and hazel eyes. She could also tell when someone was in need. She volunteered with military veterans and their families weekly.

"Nabi is technically military even though he said he hasn't seen combat since before we were born," Abby added.

"Those were the days," Miss Lily grinned.

"Ugh," Dylan, the fifteen-year-old son of Tammy and Pierce's groaned. "Is there anyone in town who meets all those requirements?"

Cassidy raised her hand. "Yes, dear?" Miss Daisy asked.

"What about Mrs. Duvall?" Cassidy said as everyone looked at each other.

"That's perfect!" Ariana squealed and jumped up.

"No, it's not," Abby called out, quieting everyone.

"Cassidy, if her name is Mrs., that means she's married already."

The Rose sisters looked at each other and clinked their glasses in celebration. "It can mean she's married," Miss Violet told them.

"Or it can mean she *was* married," Miss Daisy explained.

"Mrs. Duvall, or Grace as we know her, was married," Miss Lily told them, "but her husband died. He was more concerned with rock climbing than being a good husband."

"And four years ago he went on some major climb right after they moved here from Lexington," Miss Daisy said, picking up the story. "He was way out west while Grace was here teaching Cassidy's kindergarten class."

"That's right," Miss Violet said as she remembered the incident well. "Your daddy," she said, pointing to Sydney and Wyatt, "was the sheriff and had to tell her that her husband died when his carabiner broke near the top of the rock face."

"Grace was devastated, so we've never thought of fixing her up with Nabi or anyone else for that matter," Miss Lily told them.

"That's so sad," Sydney said and the other girls nodded.

"Maybe she's not ready to date," Jackson said.

"But she would be perfect!" Ariana protested. "Her father was in the military. She's super nice and loves kids."

"And she rides horses," Cassidy added.

"Then there's only one way to find out if they'd be perfect together," Zain said smiling.

"We need to get them together," Gabe finished.

"To the perfect wife!" Miss Lily cheered.

"Now we just need the perfect plan," Abigail said as she started to lay out her strategy with military precision.

"See, contin.., s.

Chapter Four

G race Duvall shielded her eyes from the sun as she
looked up at the group of youngsters standing in front
of her. Cassidy Davies, one of the first students she had
when she moved to Keeneston four years ago, smiled at her.
She had brought along her brothers, Jace and Dylan, and
her older sister, Piper, appeared to be stuck driving them.

"This is my friend, Ariana Ali Rahman," she said,
pointing to the auburn-haired girl. "And these are my
cousins, Reagan and Riley Davies, and my other friend,
Abigail Mueez."

Grace smiled and pulled off her gardening gloves. She
stood up from the small flowerbed she was working on and
dusted off her knees before shaking their hands.

"It's nice to meet you all. Now, what brings you here
during your summer vacation?"

"Well," Abigail said as she stepped forward, "see, we
need your help. Our really good friends, Zain and Gabe,
you know, the princes of Rahmi?"

"My brothers," Ariana added.

Grace smiled and nodded. She hadn't reached the age
of thirty-three without being able to spot something funny.
And years of teaching kindergarten told her these kids were
up to something. But for the life of her, she couldn't figure
out what it was.

they want to get a horse all on their own," Abigail
ed.

Doesn't their father own a *horse farm*?" Grace asked as
e tried not to laugh.

"Yes, but they want to do it on their own. They think
they're too big to listen to Mom and Dad anymore," Ariana
told her.

"So, what does this have to do with me?"

"Maybe I can make this simpler," eighteen-year-old
Piper started. "They're at the same barn where Cassidy said
you board your horse, and they think they found the end-
all and be-all of horses. The owner is asking $25,000 . . ."

"What?" Grace shrieked. She hated leaving Zoe there,
but it was the only place she could afford to board the
beautiful paint horse she used for barrel racing.

"See?" Piper said in typical teenage fashion. "They
think they can become overnight barrel racers, and it'll get
them girls. Boys . . ." Piper crossed her arms over her chest
and rolled her eyes.

"It's a scam, but they won't listen to us," Abigail
concluded.

"Mommy and Daddy will totally ship them back to
Rahmi for the summer if they buy those horses," Ariana
said sadly as she stuck out her bottom lip in a cute pout.

Dylan looked annoyed but started talking anyway. "So,
we need your help. Cassidy," he said giving his sister a
nudge, "said you were a barrel racer. We're hoping they'll
listen to you instead of being shipped back to Rahmi."

"Even if they act stupid, they're still our friends," Jace
said with a shrug of his shoulders, showing he was more
mature than the average twelve-year-old.

Grace nodded her head. "Give me ten minutes to get
cleaned up. God help teenage boys," she said as she tried

not to get aggravated.

She invited the kids inside and hurried to her bedroom. This was why she taught kindergarten. She was tired of boys who never matured past sixteen — like her former husband, bless his heart.

Grace and Bo had grown up in the same holler near Prestonsburg in Eastern Kentucky. They had been childhood sweethearts. She thought their relationship was romantic. He thought marrying his childhood sweetheart was a shortcut bypassing the trouble and time dating took. Grace's husband had been a good man . . . he just never matured past sixteen. He was addicted to the high of extreme physical challenges.

Growing up in the Appalachian Mountains was beautiful, but it also let Bo escape reality. He went four-wheeling instead of going to school and rock climbing instead of going to work. Because he had Grace on his side, she covered for him. She told the principal he had mono. She paid the rent on their small apartment while she went to the University of Pikeville. And she talked him into moving to Lexington so she could get a master's in education. Then, when she got her first job in Lexington and had a larger paycheck, Bo became even more adventurous.

Laying on the guilt trip that she was "too busy doing what she loved" to spend time with him, he talked her into paying for trips out west so he could go climbing. She had loved Bo so much she had gladly handed over the majority of her paycheck to give him his dream.

Then, budget cuts laid her off. She saw the advertisement for the kindergarten teacher in Keeneston and jumped on it. To celebrate, she sent Bo on his dream trip. Ten days into teaching at Keeneston Elementary

School, Sheriff Davies pulled her from her class and told her about her husband's accident. She was scared. Grace had never been alone. Sure, she was alone when he left to go climbing, but she had always been half of Grace and Bo. And now she was just Grace. She grieved for a long time as she struggled with her new reality. But three months after Bo's death, she decided she couldn't give up on life. Grace Duvall had a chance to become her own woman. It was just too bad no one had seen her as that. So she had bought her horse, Zoe, and started barrel racing.

Just the year before, she decided she was ready to start dating again. Only every man in town was so sensitive to the fact that she was a widow they didn't see her as a woman. And how was she to announce she was ready to start dating again? Just walk into the Blossom Café and tell everyone there? It wouldn't look good to announce the kindergarten teacher was ready to date—or have sex. So, she tried a dating site. That didn't go well. All she got were men who wanted to pretend they were toddlers. So Grace had given up. She raced her horse, and that was enough for now.

Grace splashed water on her face and brushed out her curly, dark brown hair before grabbing a University of Kentucky baseball cap and sticking it on. If she could talk some sense into these teenagers, she would feel like she'd made the world a better place by showing a pair of young men how to be responsible.

The group of kids still sat in the living room right where she'd left them. "Okay, let's go talk some sense into them," Grace said as she grabbed her purse.

Cassidy came up and slipped her hand into hers. "Thank you, Mrs. Duvall. I knew we could count on you."

She looked down into a set of hazel eyes that melted her

heart. Oh, she was good. They were definitely up to something; Grace just hoped it was something worthwhile.

Nabi unsaddled his horse and started to rub him down. It was nice to let go of his problems and enjoy the day with friends. Now it was time for a shower and then click Send on his email. His father would find him a wife, and within a year he would be a father. And maybe, if he were lucky, he would even have a wife he liked being around.

The sound of the barn door opening caused him to pause brushing his horse. Two people entered and stopped at the first stall to look at the horse there.

"I don't care what Dad says. I want to pick out my own horse—my own hobby."

Zain. Nabi knew his voice anywhere.

"Let's do it. There are two barrel horses out at Cross's farm that we can buy for $25,000. We'll use some of the money Grandpa left us. Mom and Dad don't have to know." Gabe sat down on a bale of hay, and Nabi could envision the pout on his face.

"Let's do it. We can be real cowboys instead of just growing up with horses. The girls at Yale will be all over us then."

"I'm in. Let's go."

Nabi shook his head. When he went out to talk some sense into the boys, they were already gone. He tossed the brush into the tack box and dusted off his jeans. It looked like Uncle Nabi was going to have to come to the rescue once again.

The drive to Cross Arrow Farm was relatively short. It bordered the west side of Mo's farm. Mr. Cross only had about fifteen acres and most of it was run-down. Nabi knew Katelyn Davies had begged her husband, Marshall to go out there many times to do wellness checks on the animals. She was sure Mr. Cross wasn't caring for them properly.

Mo and Ahmed were similarly worried. Mo had tried to buy Cross Arrow, but Mr. Cross wanted three times the fair market value. It didn't matter that Mo had the money. He refused to be taken advantage of by a creep. They were currently biding their time and waiting for Mr. Cross to move toward bankruptcy. He only had two boarders, and at the rates they were paying, Cross wouldn't be able to keep up with his mortgage. Mo's plan was to buy out the farm and rescue all the animals.

Ahmed was so worried about the horses he even ordered his farm workers to drop extra hay over the fence and to hang buckets of oats during the night so the horses didn't suffer. That's why Nabi had to stop Zain and Gabe. First, Cross's horses were in horrible condition. Second, it was common knowledge Cross had until the end of the summer to pay arrears in the amount of $25,000 to the bank or lose his farm. If Zain and Gabe were responsible for allowing him to continue to neglect his animals and stay on the farm, then he was worried what their parents would do to the kids.

As soon as Nabi pulled his black SUV to a stop in front of the falling-down barn, he knew something wasn't right. He spotted the twins' SUV and Piper's ten-year-old Ford Explorer with a Davidson College sticker; next to that was a tiny two-door sedan he didn't recognize. He parked his car, jumped out, and hurried to the dilapidated barn.

"I know we don't know each other, but if you do this it will be the biggest mistake of your life," a woman's soft, yet authoritative voice rang out through the dark barn.

Nabi's eyes hadn't adjusted to the dark inside the smelly barn, so he followed the sweet voice of the woman talking.

"What do you know about barrel horses? I'm a prince!"

Oh, Nabi was going to kick his butt. He knew Mo and Dani would be even harder on Zain if they heard that. They didn't tolerate that kind of behavior.

"Well, I guess that goes to show that wearing a crown on your head doesn't mean there's anything in it. If you think this is a good deal, then you are one very empty-minded prince. And I know plenty about barrel racing. I have a roomful of trophies to prove it. But that doesn't matter. You say you're nineteen and want to be treated like an adult. So grow up!"

Nabi's eyes widened as the group of people standing in the back of the barn grew near. He saw Zain and Gabe hang their heads and give each other one of those twin looks that meant they were communicating silently. Abby and Kale, along with Ariana and Pierce's crew, stood with their arms crossed as they watched a woman in jeans and a plaid shirt lecture the boys.

She was pretty from behind. All soft curves and shoulder-length curly hair. Nabi didn't know who she was or why she was there. Cross was an old cuss with a son down in Mississippi, but no wife or daughter that he knew of.

"You should listen to the woman. She's giving you the same advice I am going to give you, which is to grow the hell up. If you don't get your asses home right now, then I will tell your parents about the way you acted here today," Nabi said as he came to a stop behind the mystery woman.

Zain and Gabe audibly gasped. "Uncle Nabi, please don't."

33

The woman's back straightened before she turned around. He was struck by her beautiful round face. She had the high color of irritation, and he had never seen anyone who was so adorable when mad.

Nabi had to force himself to look away from the mystery woman and back to the nervous boys. "Then get home right now and never step foot on this farm again. You know how we feel about it. And when you get home, you need to head over to my barn and clean out the stalls. When you're done with that, I am sure the farm trucks need a good washing."

The twins groaned and shot looks at their sister and friends standing nearby. But Nabi didn't care about them or the way Zain, Gabe, and the rest of the kids went sulking off. All he cared about was the appreciative look in the eyes of the woman standing in front of him.

Chapter Five

Grace looked up, way up, into the most gorgeous set of whiskey-colored eyes. While Grace wasn't a shrinking violet by any means—she was five-foot-eight—this man was easily six feet tall. His seductive eyes accentuated his strong face and black hair. With a no-nonsense tone, he had sent the kids scampering with their tails tucked, all the while helping them out by not telling their parents. He was kind, fair, and didn't put up with any of their pretentious whining. And, yeah, he was drop-dead sexy.

Grace looked quickly at her worn cowboy boots, faded jeans, and button-up shirt that did nothing for her figure. She wasn't one to worry about her looks, but she was very conscious of him checking her out. She cast a quick glance at his hand and didn't see a ring on a very special finger. Her heart picked up a beat as her eyes collided with his.

"Thank you for your help. They may look like men, but they still have a lot of growing up to do." The man stuck his hands in his pockets and sent her a grin that made her forget what he was talking about. "So, do you live on the farm? I didn't know Cross had any family." The man continued to talk, and finally Grace realized he was asking her a question.

"Oh, no. I'm not related to Cross, thankfully. And you're welcome. It seems as if you, your brother, and sister-in-law are doing a good job teaching them responsibility."

He smiled again, and Grace felt heat rushing to a part of her that had been dormant a very long time. "We're not related. I'm Nabi Mosteghanemi, Dani and Mo's head of security." He held out his hand and she took it. It was warm and callused. He held her hand firmly, but the way he ran his thumb over her knuckles made Grace feel like giggling.

"Grace Duvall. It's nice to meet you."

"Likewise. So, why are you here? Not that I'm not grateful."

"Cassidy Davies was a student of mine, and she had her cousins talk me into coming over here to knock some sense into the boys. This is my horse," Grace said, smiling as she reached into her purse and pulled out an apple. She walked over to a nearby stall and snuggled up to her horse's head. Zoe nuzzled her with obvious affection and happily chewed on her snack.

"She's a beauty."

"I think so. I'm hoping I can win a few more barrel races and afford to move her to a nicer farm. See, I'm a teacher, and I don't make all that much. This is the only place I can afford to keep her for the time being."

"Get all your things. I'll not have you keeping this fine horse here," Nabi ordered.

Grace felt her hackles rising. She had been her own woman these past four years and wasn't used to taking orders. "Excuse me?"

Nabi had the grace to look embarrassed. "I'm sorry. I just hate thinking of you here. The barn looks unsafe. Not only am I fearful it'll fall on your horse, but I'm worried about you as well. Please, let me repay you for your help with Zain and Gabe by boarding your horse at Desert Sun

Farm until you find a more suitable place for her."

"Desert Sun Farm? There's no way I can afford that," Grace gasped. They had Kentucky Derby winners at that farm.

"I'm not going to charge you for it. It's a way to show my thanks. There's an empty stall right next to my horse. I'll have someone come and pick her up in twenty minutes if you will agree." Nabi reached forward and took her hand in his. "Please, Miss Duvall."

"Mrs."

"What?"

"Mrs. Duvall."

Nabi dropped her hand. "Oh, I'm sorry. I guess you'll want to confer with your husband then. But know my offer is still open."

Grace let out a deep breath. This was where all her would-be suitors ran for the hills. "My husband passed away four years ago. And thank you, I think I will take you up on the offer."

"I'll call the farm now. By the time you have everything packed up, the trailer will be here."

Grace watched as he stepped from the barn and made his call. He didn't seem to be scared about talking to her after she told him about her husband. So many men just didn't know how to act so they made excuses and ran.

She didn't know what to make of the offer to board Zoe, but she wasn't going to look a gift horse in the mouth. To have her horse in such luxury as Desert Sun Farm . . . she'd feel so secure whenever she'd leave Zoe. With her mind made up, Grace tossed all her supplies into her tack box and locked it up. There wasn't much, but she pulled her two saddles from the tack room along with the rest of her riding gear and set them down outside the barn door.

KATHLEEN BROOKS

"Here, let me help you," Nabi said as he shoved his phone into his back pocket and took the saddle from her grasp.

"Thank you. I really don't know what to say or how I can possibly repay you. The peace of mind this will give me . . ." Grace pushed the baseball cap down farther to shield her eyes from the sun.

"My pleasure. I'm sorry about your loss. Your husband, I mean."

Grace almost groaned. Now he would pity her. "Thank you."

Nabi gave her a slight nod before walking back into the barn and hefting her tack box up as if it weighed nothing. Grace felt the disappointment more than usual. She'd had hopes for this one. He was kind, strong, and compassionate. But now he seemed totally freaked out by her. The sound of a truck pulling a trailer reached her as she walked Zoe from her stall.

"Just what in the hell is going on here?" Mr. Cross yelled as he stormed up to the barn. "Where do you think you're taking that horse?"

"Zoe is coming to Desert Sun Farm," Nabi told him as Grace's view of the old crooked man disappeared behind Nabi's large shoulders.

"I can talk for myself," Grace said as she leaned around Nabi to see Mr. Cross's face turn red.

"You can't leave before the end of the year or you owe me a cancellation fee of $1000," Cross said smugly. He knew she didn't have that type of money. "And if you're boarding your horse at Desert Sun Farm, then that money shouldn't be a problem for you. Your horse doesn't leave here until you've paid it."

"I don't have that kind of money!" Grace gasped as

38

Cross made a move to grab Zoe. Zoe grew nervous and pulled back, but Nabi was there with a gentle hand to calm her.

"Let me see the boarding contract," Nabi said simply as he motioned for the workers from Desert Sun Farm to put Zoe in the trailer.

"No. It's none of your business," Cross spat.

"But it is mine," Grace said, encouraged by Nabi's thinking. She'd never been given a copy of the contract and couldn't remember what it said. "I would like to see it."

"You signed it. You should remember it," Cross said. "You owe me that money, or I'll sue you and take your horse as payment."

Nabi stepped forward and lowered his voice. "You show Mrs. Duvall that contract right now, or you won't see a dime. If you don't produce it, then any attempts to contact Mrs. Duvall will be taken as harassment, and I'll have a little talk with the sheriff about it."

Cross grunted and headed inside as Zoe was loaded into the trailer. "Thank you. I don't know what I'll do if I have to pay that money."

"I have a feeling you won't need to," Nabi said before lifting the tack box and putting it in the trailer.

Cross walked slowly from his house and with pursed lips looked up at Nabi. "I can't find the blasted thing. I guess you can take her, but I won't forget this."

Grace gulped at the underlying threat. Nabi stepped closer to him and talked. She could see his lips moving but couldn't hear what he said. She did see that Cross lost all color in his face and then shook his head before hurrying back inside.

"What was that all about?"

"Just coming to a little understanding. Now, I'll be

happy to escort you to your new stable. Just follow me." Nabi smiled as he opened the door to her car for her.

Nabi hurried around to get into his SUV. That little prick had tried to threaten her. Before he knew it, Nabi had threatened him within an inch of his miserable life. Normally, he wasn't so aggressive. But the thought of that man causing any harm to the delectable Grace Duvall set him on edge.

He looked into the rear-view mirror and saw her following him. So, she was a widow. Nabi wondered if she was dating again, or maybe she already had a boyfriend. Someone as adorably sexy as her wouldn't last long in Keeneston. The Rose sisters would have her fixed up in a second. That was too bad. Grace was the first woman to get his attention in a long time. It wasn't just her looks — it was also the way she talked, the way she cared for her horse, and the obvious way the kids liked her. It was just too bad he probably wouldn't have a chance to get to know her better.

The barn came into view as he saw Zain and Gabe tossing some hay into the stalls they had just cleaned. Interestingly enough, the others seemed to be washing the cars for them. As soon as they saw Nabi, they dropped the hose and soap and pretended to be sitting there watching Zain and Gabe clean out stalls. What was going on?

He pulled to a stop, and the trailer pulled around the parking lot and backed up to the pasture next to the barn. Nabi hopped out of the SUV and hurried to open Grace's door for her.

"Welcome to your new home . . . I mean, Zoe's new home. I'm sure you live with your boyfriend." Nabi slammed his mouth shut as Grace's eyes grew wide. Gosh, he was an idiot.

"Boyfriend? I don't have a boyfriend. Why would you think that?"

Nabi couldn't have heard her right. "You don't have a boyfriend? I just didn't think it was possible for a woman like you to be single."

"I'm sure your girlfriend wouldn't like you talking like that." Grace blushed.

"He doesn't have a girlfriend," Abby shouted from where they were hanging out by the barn doors.

Nabi didn't know what to say. Apparently Grace didn't either since they both stood staring at each other, not saying a word.

"Mrs. Duvall, what is Zoe doing here?" Cassidy asked as she broke their stares.

"Mr. Nabi invited Zoe to stay here for a little while. Wasn't that nice of him?"

Cassidy nodded. "Uncle Nabi is nice like that."

"That's right. He always looks out for everyone," Abby chimed in.

"Whether we like it or not," Zain groaned.

"But we always appreciate it," Gabe said as he elbowed his brother in the side.

"Uncle Nabi is the best," Ariana smiled as she ran up and gave him a hug.

"Yeah, he's the coolest," Kale said. "He once taught me how to hack the . . ."

Nabi cleared his throat. "Thank you for that. What has gotten into you guys today?"

Innocent faces all stared back at him. "Well, it is your birthday," Piper said quickly to fill the silence.

"It's your birthday?" Grace asked. Nabi nodded, not taking his eyes off the kids. They were up to something. "And you spent your afternoon helping me instead of relaxing and enjoying your day. I just love birthdays. I don't know how to thank you for all you've done."

"You could bake him a birthday cake," Cassidy suggested.

"Or cook him dinner," Piper added.

"Girls," Nabi said with censure in his voice.

"No, that's a great idea." Grace smiled. "I would love to have you come to my house for dinner. But I'm sure you have other plans."

"He doesn't," Dylan jumped in.

"Great!" Grace beamed and Nabi felt his heart flip in his chest. "How about seven?"

"That is very kind of you. I look forward to it," Nabi said with more excitement than he meant to show. "Well, I'll let you get settled. I'll see you tonight."

Nabi walked calmly to the SUV and didn't breathe until the barn was out of sight. He had four hours until dinner, and he hadn't a clue what to do. He hadn't been on a date in a long time. The time he spent with women usually involved starting at a bar and leaving her house before morning. He needed help.

Chapter Six

"You have a date?" Ahmed asked as he watched the newest batch of three-year-olds gallop around the practice track at the back of the farm.

"Yes. What do I do?"

"What do you mean, what do you do?"

"What do I wear, what do I talk about? Do I bring something with me?"

"What kind of date is it?" Mo asked.

Nabi thought for a second and then his shoulders slumped. "A pity date."

"A pity date?" Will Ashton, former NFL quarterback and co-owner of one of the horses they were training, asked.

"Yeah. I helped her out with old Cross. I'm letting her board her horse next to mine, and he tried to get her to pay $1000 for breaking their supposed contract. He threatened to keep her horse if she didn't pay. I put a stop to it, and then the kids told her it was my birthday, so I think she did it just out of pity since I had no plans."

Ahmed, Mo, and Will exchanged glances and shrugged.

"Nothing wrong with that," Will said.

"Yeah, you have to get your foot in the door somehow," Ahmed told him.

"I don't know. It's been forever since I dated. But it

seems to me a pity date would be coffee or something that didn't last long. A home-cooked meal seems pretty intimate to me," Mo said as he clicked his stopwatch when their stallion crossed the finish line. He showed it to Will who just smiled.

"That's true. We aren't really up to date on this kind of thing. I guess we could ask Sienna," Will said.

Nabi cringed at the thought of asking Will's oldest child, who was no longer much of a child. "No way. I would sooner ask Ryan, but that is not going to happen." Nabi shook his head. Talk about pathetic.

"Then we could ask the next best thing." Will pulled out his cell phone. "Cole, it's Will. I'm over at the track at Desert Sun Farm. Nabi has been invited out to dinner with some woman. Has Ryan mentioned anything about dating?"

Nabi covered his face with his hands. Could this get any more embarrassing?

"Cole's calling the guys, and they're on their way over," Will informed them.

Nabi had his answer. Yes, it could get more embarrassing.

Grace kicked off her dusty cowboy boots and turned on the shower. She unbuttoned her shirt and tossed it into the hamper. Taking a deep breath, she looked at herself in her bathroom mirror as she reached for her toothbrush. Kinda flat-ish stomach, breasts a B cup, strong, muscled thighs from riding . . .

"What have I gotten myself into?" she groaned.

Grace walked to her closet and pulled out a cute wispy

skirt that made her feel young again. It stopped above her knees and was the kind of skirt she used to twirl around the room in when she was a child. She pulled out an ivory lace top and put them both on the bed. She could do this. It was just dinner . . . at her house . . . with the sexiest man she'd ever laid eyes on.

Grace fell back onto her bed and closed her eyes. Nabi was so out of her league. She hadn't been on a real date since she was a kid. Bo had been her only boyfriend and they didn't "date" at that age anyway.

She stepped into the shower. Should she talk about the weather? Or maybe ask about the weather in Rahmi? She'd never been there and didn't know much about that small island country in the Middle East. As important as Nabi was to the prince, she was sure he had a lot of interesting stories to tell. But what did she have to offer someone like that? She was just a kindergarten teacher. Granted, there was nothing better than the feeling of accomplishment when a student learned to read and write, but would a man who was into personal security want to know about that?

She turned off the water, stepped out of the shower, and dressed. She was about to dry her hair when there was a knock on the door. She shot a glance at the clock and cursed. He couldn't be this early! She hurried to the door and nervously opened it.

"Hello, dear," Miss Lily said sweetly.

Grace smiled at Miss Lily and her two sisters who stood on her tiny porch. "Hi, ladies. What a surprise. Is there something I can do for you? Please, come in."

Grace opened the door wider and stepped back to allow the elderly sisters to slowly walk inside.

"Thank you. We don't want to take up too much of your time," Miss Violet said as she patted Grace's cheek.

"Don't you look lovely."

"Thank you." Grace gave each sister a hug. It was hard not to with these three.

"Aren't you sweet?" Miss Daisy set a large pitcher on the kitchen table.

"We made a big batch of iced tea and realized we made way too much. We thought you might want some," Miss Lily said as she gestured to the large pitcher.

"Thank you. That's very kind of you. Your iced tea is the best," Grace said. Relief coursed through her. She could serve it at dinner tonight. She could only make regular from-a-box iced tea, but the Rose sisters' tea was the stuff of dreams. And tonight she needed all the help she could get to impress Nabi.

"You're welcome. It's a very special batch of tea," Miss Daisy told her as the three sisters shared a look.

"I appreciate it. I must admit my iced tea isn't up to your caliber."

"We know," Miss Violet said cheerfully.

"Well, we must be going. Father James is having bingo at the church. Enjoy the special tea," Miss Lily called over her shoulder as the sisters shuffled out as quickly as they had arrived.

Grace shook her head but before she could think more of it, the oven went off. It was time to get her cakes out.

"You want to know how to date?" Cy, a stuntman super-spy turned farmer asked, and Nabi groaned, again.

"It shouldn't be too hard. We all dated our wives. How much can change in twenty years?" Miles asked with a shrug.

"I don't know. Ryan talks about rules. Were there rules when we dated? I just remember trying not to piss y'all off so I could keep sleeping with Paige," Cole Parker, the head of the Lexington FBI Office, told them.

"I don't care that you've been married and had children with my sister; they are the result of immaculate conceptions as far as I'm concerned," Pierce, inventor extraordinaire, said with a shudder.

"I overheard Sydney complaining that some guy at college only talked about himself. So, you should probably ask her lots of questions," Marshall, the Sheriff of Keeneston, put in.

Cade nodded his agreement. "Yeah, and listen. Sophie complained some guy she went out with was too busy on his cell phone to listen to her."

"Layne complained about a date trying to be all macho — ordering for her when she didn't want him to, telling her what to drink, and talking about how badass he was at the gym," Miles growled. "Needless to say, she set him straight. Maybe tone down the whole big bad soldier thing."

"That's good." Pierce snapped his fingers. "Go with all the good things you've done. Piper really liked this one guy who showed his *sensitive* side. But not too much, just a little."

Cy nodded. "I'd leave out the explosions, shootings, and fighting until the third date at least."

"Wait a second, you all didn't do any of these things with your wives," Nabi pointed out.

They all looked at each other and shrugged. "True, which is why we had to spy on our kids to find out how dating is done," Will replied for the group.

"I'm sure this is real good intel then," Nabi said,

frowning.

"Oh, it's solid intel. You think we'd let our daughters date without knowing about every single thing that went on? Shoot, I have Reagan and Riley's phones tapped. Just don't tell Gemma." Cy lowered his voice and looked around as if his wife, Gemma, a newspaper reporter and novelist, might suddenly appear.

Cade similarly looked around for his wife, a former DEA agent turned sheriff's deputy. "Don't tell Annie, but I hack into Sophie's phone and email, too. You know, just to make sure she's safe."

"I may or may not have answered the door to all of Sydney's dates wearing my sheriff's uniform and carrying a gun," Marshall said innocently.

"I might have tampered with a date's sports car so Piper could drive her car instead. What?" Pierce asked as Nabi shook his head. "As if I would trust a teenage boy in a sports car to drive my daughter around."

"I had the whole offensive line from my old NFL team show up the first time Sienna brought a boy to dinner. I might have whispered that they like to break little boys who hurt my daughter," Will said with pride.

Miles nodded. "I mentioned I knew twenty-three ways to kill someone with my bare hands during my introduction to Layne's date."

Nabi's eyes went wide. "What did she do?"

"Layne? She shrugged and said if the boy was too much of a wimp to meet me then he wasn't the boy for her. Have I mentioned I have a great wife who taught my daughter about men?" Miles smiled.

The rest of the men all nodded as they agreed that their wives were fantastic.

"It's the only thing that keeps me sane. Knowing Annie

taught Sophie all she knows. It doesn't mean I don't still check up on her, though," Cade, the head football coach at Keeneston High School, said seriously. He would never admit that while Sophie was in high school, he told his team that if anyone tried to date her he would make them run sprints until they lost all interest in dating.

"Has this helped at all?" Mo asked.

"It has helped me decide Abigail doesn't need to date yet," Ahmed mumbled.

"It's taught me that I'll never spy on my daughter," Nabi said as he shook his head at his friends, who in turn just laughed at him.

"You'll be worse than all of us. Just you wait and see," Cy said as he slapped Nabi on his back.

"Let's see if I can just get through this date first. Thanks, guys." Nabi waved as his friends went on laughing at the idea of Nabi not overprotecting any daughters he might have.

Chapter Seven

Grace took one last look in the mirror and opened the front door. Nabi stood smiling at her with a handful of daffodils. He was dressed casually in jeans and a white button-up shirt with the sleeves rolled up to expose tanned, muscled arms.

"These are for you. Thank you for inviting me to dinner tonight," Nabi said as he held the flowers out to her.

"Some say daffodils represent chivalry and new beginnings." Grace smiled as she put her nose to the delicate pedals and took a quick sniff. She could have sworn his cheeks flushed as he looked at the floor quickly.

"Please come in. Dinner is ready. I hope fried catfish is okay with you."

"Sounds wonderful. And smells wonderful, too."

Grace led Nabi to her small kitchen and reached up for a vase. Nabi looked around and then walked over to the counter. "Would you like me to pour the iced tea?"

"Yes, thank you."

Grace set the flowers on the kitchen table and served dinner. Nabi didn't talk, but she didn't mind. She was too nervous to talk anyway. At least the silence wasn't awkward. She found it strange that they seemed to be able to work together to get dinner on the table as if they had done it a thousand times.

Finally sitting down, they raised their glasses of iced tea. "To a new friend, a hero of horses, and the birthday boy. Cheers." Grace looked at the amused smile on Nabi's face and downed the Rose sisters' iced tea. He was definitely not a boy; why had she said that?

Grace coughed. The iced tea was strong. What had the Roses put in it? Nabi smiled and looked at the pitcher. "I see the Rose sisters made their special brew."

"They did say it was special. It kind of burns. What do they put in it?"

"Bourbon."

Grace's eyes went wide as her body got warm. "That explains the floating feeling. I don't drink . . . ever."

Nabi raised his glass in silent toast. "Then this should really be a party tonight."

Grace giggled. And she giggled again. Once she started, she couldn't stop. "That's funny, and this tea is yummy." Grace poured another glass and took a bite of dinner. Dinner was awesome. She was an awesome cook. Nabi was an awesome man who she bet would look awesome naked.

"Tell me about yourself. Where do you come from? Have you always wanted to be a teacher?"

Warm fuzzies overtook Grace, and she felt herself relax. "I'm from Prestonsburg. I'm an only child and always wished for siblings. When my parents divorced, I sort of adopted all my friends' younger siblings and fell into a teacher role with them. I knew by the time I was in the fourth grade I wanted to be a teacher. I wanted to be someone reliable and caring for young kids. So many of them don't have that at home."

Nabi nodded and took another drink of the spiked tea. He looked across the table as Grace animatedly told of her love of teaching and smiled. She was beautiful, intelligent, and caring. Where had she been all these years?

"And then my husband died, and these kids became even more to me. My job was my life."

Ah, that's where she'd been — grieving. Was he the test-the-waters guy, or was she only inviting him to dinner to be nice? He watched Grace take a big gulp of tea. She didn't cough this time. Instead her cheeks had a cute flush to them, and her eyes sparkled as she talked even faster while waving her hands around.

"But then I wanted to start dating, and no one would come near me. I mean, are widows really that scary? No one in town dared ask me out so I had to go online. Have you ever done online dating? No, you wouldn't need to. I mean, you're so hot and I'm so not. And so many of my friends found love online that it gave me hope. It seemed not to be, though. I did get an offer to spank a man with a ruler, though," Grace tipsily rambled on.

Nabi coughed to hide his surprise and amusement. Some people got mean when they drank. Some got tired. Some got touchy-feely. Grace got animated. She was excited, and mixed with her nervousness, she was talking with her whole body. Her eyes went big, her hands played charades, and her mouth . . . her mouth was utterly kissable.

"There's one thing wrong about what you said. You are very attractive. As for the ruler . . ."

Sienna Ashton parked her car a block away from Mrs. Duvall's house. She cut the engine and pulled up the black hoodie. She walked down the street and stopped short of the house where Nabi's SUV was parked. She glanced around and quickly ducked behind the hedgerow, making her way down the row until she had a good view of the kitchen.

A hand snaked out from the night and covered her mouth. Sienna let out a scream, but the hand muffled the noise. She was brought up tight against a hard muscled chest with strong arms holding her to him.

"It's me," a deep voice whispered in her ear. "Now stop screaming."

Who was it? *It's me* could be anyone. She nodded her head. As soon as he lowered his hand, she turned and connected with a left hook to his jaw. Before she could celebrate the victory over her mystery attacker, her arms were wrenched behind her, and her face was shoved into the ground.

"What the hell was that for?"

Sienna would have cried out, but the pressure he put on her arm could pop it out of its socket at any time.

"Don't hurt me, please."

"You idiot, I told you it was me."

Sienna tired to stay calm. She took a shaky breath. "Me who?"

"Me, Ryan. I thought you'd know my voice by now. You've only known me twenty years." He dropped her arm and turned back to the window.

"Ryan? What are you doing here? And for your information, your voice is a lot deeper now than when we grew up together." *And sexier.* "Where did you learn how to do that?"

Ryan made a disgruntled noise and refused to look at her. It was hard with her striking green eyes and light red hair. "You do know my parents, right? I know more self-defense and have more weapons training than most police officers. Not too bad for a little kid, huh? As for what I'm doing here, Zain and Gabe got stuck at a family dinner and wanted me to come spy on the happy couple. What are you doing here?"

"Abigail is at the same dinner. She texted me to see if I could spy on them. I guess since we're in college, we can get out of our houses easier. So, what have I missed?" Ryan had always been a love-struck puppy following her around. After being away at college for four years, she came back to see he had changed. Tonight was the first time she'd opened her eyes and seen him for the man he was turning into—a sexy badass.

"The Rose sisters dropped off some of their special tea. Mrs. D has had three glasses. She's plastered, and Nabi is highly amused. I've never seen him smile so much. Can't blame him, though. Mrs. D has that sexy girl-next-door thing going for her."

Sienna didn't know why, but the thought of Ryan finding Mrs. Duvall attractive irritated her. Ryan had bugged her her entire life by either trying to steal kisses or asking her to school dances. Lately he wasn't, and she actually missed it.

"Wait, they're getting up." Sienna watched as the couple moved toward the front of the house. She and Ryan crawled quietly along the hedgerow to follow them, then stopped and stretched up to look into the living room window.

Grace was in love. This man was smokin' hot. He listened. His smile sent her heart jumping from her chest. When he placed his hand at the small of her back, she thought she might just rip her clothes off right then and beg him to take her. She was so hot. Why was it so hot in here? Grace fanned her flushed face and took a seat on the couch.

Nabi sat next to her, and their legs pressed against each

other. Tearing off her clothes was *so* going to happen. She looked at his smile and then let her eyes drop lower. She would do a once-over real quick-like. He wouldn't even know she was checking him out.

Nabi held down the laugh trying to break free. Grace's mouth was slightly open as her eyes traveled down his chest and stopped at his lap. But when she licked her lips as she continued to stare, he felt himself respond instantly. He shouldn't have let her continue drinking. Now there was no hope of sleeping with her tonight. But he had to find out if she was still mourning her late husband. So, he'd plied her with the drink and interrogated her.

What he found out was that she was kind, loving, and had been walked on by her husband. She no longer mourned him. Instead of grieving him, she had decided to become her own person. Now she longed to love and to be loved. Just like him. He had listened to her repeat the feelings he had every day.

When he had determined her mind and her heart were ready to date again, he'd turned the questions to getting to know her better. Of course, he knew a lot of it from the background check he'd run on her, but it was fun to listen to her life story. They had a lot in common—fathers in the military, love of the outdoors and horses, the desire to have a family. After all this time, hope was finally blooming . . . along with something else. She really had to stop looking at his erection and licking her lips.

"What is she staring at?" Sienna whispered.

"If you don't know, then you're the kid here," Ryan shot back.

"What?"

"You don't even realize you're doing it, do you? No, you're the oldest and all high and mighty," Ryan said bitterly.

"That's not fair. I am the oldest, but I don't see what that has to do with anything."

Ryan clenched his jaw. "Now you don't care about age." He was pissed. He was still fuming at Sienna saying she saw him as a kid. Her brother, Carter, had been right. He was pathetic, and he was done with the obsession.

"What's gotten into you, Ryan?" Sienna hissed. "Oh, look! He's going to kiss her."

Ryan looked through the window and saw Nabi staring at Grace's mouth. By the way she was licking her lips, Ryan was looking at her mouth, too. Suddenly, fourteen years didn't seem like much of a gap. If Nabi backed out, then he needed someone to make him forget about the woman kneeling next to him.

He could see Nabi flex his hands into fists over and over again as if he were trying to stop himself from doing what both he and Sienna knew he was going to do. Ryan saw the moment Nabi gave in. He reached for Grace, putting one finger under her chin and raising her eyes to his. He leaned forward and they were lost in each other.

Sienna held her breath. She shouldn't be watching this. She felt her cheeks flush and was suddenly very aware of Ryan next to her. They were thigh-to-thigh and shoulder-to-shoulder as they peeked into the window. Her breathing quickened and she tried to hide it, but Ryan shot her a quick look.

Oh goodness. Those hazel eyes, that dark hair she wanted to run her hands through . . . and when did those jeans start fitting him like that?

"Damn it," Ryan cursed. He grabbed her then and crushed his mouth on hers. She felt her breasts press against his hard chest, and her hands went to his hair. She had thought the kiss would be bruising, but it wasn't. It was demanding, but Ryan seemed to caress her everywhere. Her head spun from it, and then she was set aside. She felt empty. She felt as if her world had been turned upside down and she'd die if he didn't touch her again.

"Ryan?" Sienna blinked her eyes open to find him staring down at her.

"Sorry, Sienna. But I think I've finally outgrown you." And then he was gone.

Chapter Eight

N abi groaned as Grace ran her hands over his chest. He couldn't get enough of her. He had to feel her, all of her. But when her hands reached for the very visible bulge in his pants, he knew he had to stop. He had plied her with alcohol and interrogated her. If they were going to start a real relationship, then their first time wasn't going to be groping each other on the couch like a couple of teenagers.

"Grace," he whispered as he nibbled her lip, "we need to slow down."

"Screw that." Grace yanked off her shirt and Nabi's eyes went wide. He'd never seen a more beautiful woman.

Before he knew it, he was reaching for her. Her breasts filled his hands and her head rolled back. He bent forward and placed a kiss on the base of her throat. No. He had to stop.

Nabi jumped from the couch and threw the blanket that rested on the arm at her. "Let's watch a movie."

"A movie, huh? Want to make one instead?" Grace purred as she stood up and slowly unzipped her skirt. She'd gone from excited drunk to seductive drunk real fast.

"Grace, you're drunk. As much as I would love to do that with you, I want both of us to be able to remember it the next morning."

"Oh, I'll remember it. And morning sex. We'll have it,

right? Do you know how long it's been since I've had sex?" Grace asked as she sat down to peel off her cowboy boots. Nabi watched as she tried and tried to get the first one off. "It won't stay still. Silly boot, stop moving."

Her eyes fluttered closed, and her hands stilled on her boot. Her body swayed and then slowly fell onto the couch. She'd passed out. Grace would never forgive him if she found out he kept topping off her drink to get information out of her. He may have ruined the most perfect date he'd ever had. Good thing it was his job to keep secrets, and he was very good at his job.

He let out a frustrated sigh as he picked her up from the couch. He looked down at her lacy underwear and cursed. He carried her to her bedroom and laid her on the bed, pulled off her boots, and rummaged through her drawers until he found a T-shirt to pull on over her head.

Turning back the covers, he picked her up again and placed her head on the pillow. A cute soft snore came from her, and he smiled. Nothing had ever been as endearing as her letting loose with everything she'd bottled up over the years. Grace Duvall was full of strength, hope, love, a wicked sense of humor, and the Rose sisters' special tea.

Nabi leaned down and placed a soft kiss on her cheek. "Tomorrow I'll be as honest with you as you've been with me. I promise." And for the first time, he left a date with the hope of seeing the woman again. Maybe he would wait another day to send that email to his father.

"Daddy, please?" Abby begged.

"No. You are not going to that party. You are way too young." Ahmed shook his head and clenched his teeth.

"Mom, talk to him. I'm almost sixteen, and everyone is going to be there. Zain and Gabe are going. Ryan and Jackson. Sienna and Carter. Sophie. Layne. Piper and Dylan. Reagan and Riley. Sydney and Wyatt." Abby ticked the names off her fingers.

"Where is it?" Bridget asked with motherly patience.

"It's in the field by the water tower. It's a field party. Everyone is just parking their trucks, putting the tailgates down, and hanging out."

"There will be drinking," Ahmed pointed out.

Abby rolled her eyes. "Duh. But that doesn't mean I'll drink. And Zain and Gabe said they would take me and bring me home."

Her father stared at her before motioning for her mother to follow him into their bedroom. Abby waited impatiently. She crossed her fingers. "Please, please, please," she chanted softly.

The door opened and her parents walked out together. Her father didn't look happy. That gave her some hope.

"You can go with conditions," her father said.

"Yes! Thank you, Mom!" Abby hugged her mom and smiled at them both.

"Don't thank me," Bridget said with a tight smile on her face. "It was your father's idea. I wanted to wait a little longer. This is your first and only chance to prove you're mature enough to handle this type of party."

"Yes, ma'am," Abby said seriously. When her parents gave her a chance, she knew she better not mess up. They were trusting her, and she would prove to them that they could do so.

"As I was saying, conditions," her father started. He held up a finger. "One—no drinking, smoking, or drugs. Two—you answer every call or text from us immediately.

Three—you call us anytime you feel uncomfortable. You won't be in trouble; we just want to make sure you're safe. We will pick you up immediately. And four—you are home by eleven. If Zain and Gabe won't bring you home, then remember condition number three."

"Deal," Abby squealed as she jumped up and down and threw her arms around her father. "Thank you!"

Abby pulled out her phone and sent a text to Zain and Gabe to come pick her up. They were leaving in five minutes. "I have to get ready!"

Abby ran upstairs and into her room. She brushed her hair and looked at the outfit she was wearing. Jean shorts and cowboy boots and a tank top with "Kentucky Girl" written across it. Soon, she heard Zain and Gabe knocking and knew she didn't have time to change. Her first field party! She swiped on some lip gloss and ran downstairs to hear the end of her mom lecturing Zain and Gabe.

"Yes, ma'am," they both said at the same time.

"Ready?" Zain asked.

"Yep," Abby said as she grabbed her Keeneston High School sweatshirt from the chair.

"Eleven. Not a minute later or I swear I will send your father after you," Bridget said seriously. "Now, have fun." She smiled.

Abby hugged her mom and kissed her dad before racing out the door. She jumped into the back of Zain's SUV and could hardly contain the squeal of excitement.

"Thank you, guys, so much."

"No problem, but we promised your mom and dad we'd look after you. So, no disappearing with Corey," Zain lectured.

Gabe grunted, and she thought she heard him mumble, "Tool."

Abby just smiled. Getting her first kiss was not breaking any of the conditions her father had outlined, so Zain and Gabe could just get over it. Better to ask forgiveness than permission in this case. Her phone buzzed and she smiled as she read the text from Corey. He was looking forward to talking to her tonight. Talking was not what she had in mind, but it was a good sign.

Ahmed turned to his wife after he watched the taillights disappear into the night. He did not know what possessed him to allow Abby to go when his beautiful wife was so against it. No, he knew. He was the tough dad, always the one who kept Abby in line. For once, he wanted to be the good guy. That was not something he was used to.

"I can't believe you let her go," his wife said with surprise and a little worry in her voice.

Ahmed turned and looked into Bridget's face. They'd been married for almost eighteen years, and he loved her more every day. And he'd also learned her looks. The one she was giving him at that moment said he had made a mistake, but now he had to live with it. But it wasn't a mistake to let Abby go to a party.

"With tons of boys, alcohol, and probably drugs," Bridget said with a raised eyebrow.

Maybe it was a mistake. She was just a teenager, and there would be boys trying to give her beer and . . . No. He didn't make mistakes.

"Are you now wondering if you made the right decision?"

Bridget slipped her arm into Ahmed's and walked with him back into the house. He was Ahmed. He didn't question decisions he made. With a gulp, he turned to his wife. "Honey, get the drone."

"No problem; I assume you want the small one that is the quietest," Bridget said with a smirk as she headed for the basement.

"Abs! Over here," Dylan shouted as soon as she opened the car door. It was hard to miss Dylan. Some people had started calling him Devil Davies because of his dark, brooding looks. He was fifteen, but he looked twenty and was the spitting image of his Uncle Miles — tall, muscular, dark-haired, and with the Davies signature hazel eyes. He was already over six feet tall and was intense.

The field was packed. Trucks formed a circle around the water tower. Music boomed on the speakers and coolers sat in the grass next to each back tire. Dylan and the rest of the crew from their Nabi plot were clustered around Ryan's truck. The three of them headed over and Abby felt bad she had forgotten about Nabi and Grace in her excitement.

"How did it go?" she asked Sienna who seemed to be trying to get near Ryan.

"It seemed to go really well. I kissed . . . they kissed and then we left. So, if there are no mixed signals, I think it's promising," Sienna told them.

"Unless she doesn't know what she wants. You know how fast women can change their minds," Ryan said as he took a step away from Sienna.

Carter looked between his sister and Ryan and narrowed his eyes. "What's going on?"

"Nothing," Ryan shrugged as he moved to pick up a beer from the cooler.

Abby looked at Sienna who was watching Ryan bend over the cooler as she nibbled her lower lip. Something weird was going on.

"But it looks like our mission was accomplished?"

Abby asked, drawing everyone's attention away from Ryan and Sienna.

"Looks like it." Sydney smiled.

"I'm glad. I would hate to see Nabi marry out of desperation instead of love," Reagan said while Riley nodded her agreement.

"Me too," Sophie added as she grabbed a beer from the cooler as well.

"Well, now that the mission is over, I'm off to party," Piper said before giving everyone a wave and heading to a nearby truck where a bunch of girls were dancing to country music.

"Good job, Abby. I'm glad it all worked out." Layne gave her a hug and headed over to meet with some of the girls on her volleyball team.

As the girls drifted off to hang with their friends, Abby looked around for Corey. She spotted some kids from her class Dylan was hanging with but didn't see Corey's blond locks.

"What's gotten into you?" Wyatt asked Ryan as he pulled a second beer from Ryan's hand.

"Yeah, you have to slow down or Mom and Dad will be pissed to discover you drunk," Jackson warned.

"Give me your keys." Zain's authoritative order produced instant results as Ryan handed the keys to him. Zain handed them to Jackson who pocketed them.

"You know I was just teasing you about Sienna, right?" Carter asked slowly. "Is that what's got you in a mood?"

Ryan shook his head. "No, you weren't. I was pathetically in love with her, and she thought of me as a little kid. A kid! Do I look like a kid? For crying out loud, I'm only a year younger than her; I'm a good six inches taller, have straight As in college, and nabbed a select internship with the government. But I'm just a kid," Ryan spat in disgust.

"I'm sure she didn't mean it like that," Carter defended.

"I'm sure I don't give a shit anymore."

"Ryan," Gabe said as he slapped his back, "women are strange creatures. They are deep and as you peel away the layers . . ."

"Oh stuff it, Gabe," Ryan growled.

Carter shook his head. "I'm going to find my sister."

"Ryan?" A soft voice called from behind.

Abby looked behind him and saw a pretty girl who was in the class behind Ryan's during high school.

"Want to go grab a drink and hang out?"

Ryan reached into the cooler and snagged two bottles of beer. "I would love to." Ryan smiled as he slipped an arm around her waist.

The small group watched as he headed off with the girl into the darkness. Jackson shook his head. "That's Ashley. She's had a crush on him for years."

"Abby?"

Abby spun around and came face to chest with Corey. He was here! Her heart sped up and she felt her fingers itch to touch him. "Hi, Corey."

She could practically hear the eye rolls from the boys behind her, but she ignored them. The little scene she'd just watched between them showed her they didn't know anything about relationships.

"So, you want a beer?" Corey asked as he held up a can.

"No, she doesn't," Wyatt said stiffly as he stepped up next to her.

"I didn't know you were her brother," Corey sneered.

"He's not," Abby said quickly.

"Think of all of us as her brothers," Zain and Gabe said

as they stepped forward. "Older, bigger brothers."

"Guys," Abby warned. "Let's go, Corey. They're just messing around." Abby slipped her hand into his and walked off in the direction Ryan and Ashley had gone.

"I'm so glad you're here tonight," Corey purred as they found a spot under a willow tree. Abby looked around at the canopy of leaves and felt as if they were in their own world. Music strummed in the distance and mixed with the sound of a nearby stream. It was so romantic — perfect for her first kiss.

"Me, too."

Corey set down his beer and scooted closer to her. She swore her heart would leap from her chest at any second.

"I've wanted to do this forever," he said softly as he reached out and pulled her against him.

"Then what's stopping you?" Abby challenged.

Corey pressed his lips to hers and her heart stopped beating. She was shocked at how it hurt. He ground his lips hard against hers. She tried to pull back a little to coax him into slowing down. His grip tightened on her arms as he held her tight against him.

"Whoa," Abby panted as she pulled her head back.

"I know, right? It's so intense." Corey licked his lips and ran his hand down her back before moving his hand to her stomach.

"No. I mean, easy. We can go slow, you know?"

"So, you're a tease," Corey snapped.

"What? No, I just meant let's kiss a little softer and slower." Abby felt the mood and the excitement flee. Why was Corey acting like this? "Let's talk a bit. What are you up to this summer?"

"Talk? I didn't ask you out here to talk."

"Well, I didn't come to be pawed at," Abby snapped.

Corey took a deep breath. "You're right. Let me try again."

Corey leaned forward and placed a soft kiss on her lips. Okay, that was pleasant even if Corey was acting like Ryan. Maybe men really didn't understand women. Corey put his lips to hers softly. Oh, this was what kissing was all about. She felt herself flush as Corey ran his hand down her back to cup her hip and pull her closer. She felt the pressure increase as he became more demanding. She pulled back to slow him down as he thrust his tongue in her mouth. Eww. It was so . . . wet.

She pushed against his chest to let him know he'd gone far enough. Instead of slowing him down, it encouraged him. She pulled her head to the side to dislodge him. "Stop!"

"You are a tease," he said as a curse.

Abby felt her heart start to race for a whole different reason. Her friends had been right. Corey was a tool, a player, and an asshole . . . an asshole with a very strong grip on her.

"I said no! If you treasure your balls, then you'll let me go right now," Abby said with barely controlled anger. But when his hand moved to squeeze her breast, she'd had enough of being nice. A swift uppercut to his chin made him freeze in place. He looked surprised, and then his eyes rolled slowly back into his head. The branches from the willow tree parted as Zain, Gabe, Jackson, and Wyatt looked on. They saw Abby's angry face and Corey's hand on her breast. Then Corey fell to the ground with a thud.

"Abby, why don't you come with me? I think some of the girls were asking where you were," Jackson said, holding out his hand to her.

Abby smiled. They were too loyal to say, "I told you

so." With a sigh of relief, she reached up and took Jackson's hand. He held open the curtain of branches for her and escorted her from the tree.

"Wake up, dickhead," she heard Wyatt demand and then heard the hard slap of a hand against a face. He was so handsome that sometimes it was easy to forget Wyatt had a backbone of steel that he inherited from his father, Marshall, who was a member of Special Forces.

"What?" Corey said groggily. "What . . . that bitch punched me!"

"Oh yeah? What until you see what we do to you," Gabe said with a tone that sent chills down Abby's back.

"I warned you we were like her brothers," Zain snarled. "And we protect our own."

"Cross or uppercut?" Jackson, in his normal quiet and in control way, smiled down to her as he led her away.

"Uppercut."

"Good girl." Jackson patted her hand at the same time the sound of a fist connecting with a stomach reached her ears.

"Now, let me teach you a little about respecting a woman," Wyatt's slow drawl said from behind her. Abby didn't hear any more as Jackson carried on a line of soothing small talk. Soon they reached his truck, and he handed her a cold beer.

"For your hand, not for you to drink." Abby looked down and saw a slight swelling of her knuckles. She'd hit lots of people in karate tournaments, but this was the first time she'd done it without pads. The cold can felt good on her hand.

"Thank you."

"Anytime. I'm going to hate when Greer starts to date. Luckily, my parents are a lot like yours. She'll know how to take care of herself. I just hate that she might have to."

"I should have listened to you all."

"You're right, you should have," Zain said from behind her.

Abby turned to see Zain, Gabe, and Wyatt walking up to her. They wore grim expressions, and suddenly Abby felt like crying.

"I'm so sorry."

"Don't be sorry," Wyatt said gently.

"It wasn't your fault. It was his." Gabe pulled her into a hug. "Are you okay?"

"Yes. I stopped it as soon as I realized he wasn't listening to me. I had just wanted my first kiss to be so much better than that. I mean, that was horrible and slobbery. And he had bad breath."

"Come on," Jackson smiled. "It's your first field party. What would it be like if you didn't dance barefoot in a field to country music?"

Abby felt the disappointment fall away as Jackson led her to where a group of people danced in the center of the circle of trucks. Soon she was laughing as she danced with all her friends. She even danced with Nolan from her class. He had always been shy and stuttered his request to dance. But as soon as she said yes, his smiled warmed her instantly.

The song ended, and Abby didn't want to leave Nolan's arms. He held her gently. He made her laugh, and he had even asked for her phone number. Who knew the quiet guy in science class was so nice? And cute. He was tall, a little on the skinny side, but his deep-green eyes were intense.

"Abby, time to go," Zain called from behind her.

"Sorry, I have to go. Curfew," Abby said sadly. Corey hadn't reappeared. In fact, she'd forgotten all about him.

"Me, too. My parents want me home by eleven. I'll text you later, if that's okay?"

"That would be great. Thanks for the dance, Nolan."

Zain smiled at Nolan and shook his hand before they each went their separate ways. All the way home Gabe ribbed Zain about a girl he danced with. Abby only half-listened. Tonight she'd learned something she never wanted to admit. Her mom had told her the flashy bad-boy types were trouble. It was the strong silent ones who were the keepers. Tonight she'd realized her mother was right. It was a sickening feeling to admit her mother was right but a comfort to know she would always be there to give advice.

Chapter Nine

G race felt the throbbing before she opened her eyes. The world tilted slightly when she sat up. She looked down at herself and cringed. She was in a T-shirt and tucked into bed. The only clue that it hadn't been of her own doing was that she still wore a bra. She hated them, so it would have been off immediately if she had undressed herself. And that meant her first date in years had undressed her and tucked her into bed.

Grace fell back onto the bed and felt like crying. He would never call her and ask for a second date. What an idiot she was. The tea . . . the blasted special tea. It tasted so good, and she had been so nervous. The tea had made her relax. She didn't even want to know what she had said. She remembered talking, getting up to go to the living room, and the kiss. Wow, that kiss had rocked her world. Then things got a little fuzzy. She just hoped she didn't do anything to embarrass herself too badly.

A knock at the door made her grab her head. Who in the world was here so early? She rolled out of bed and stumbled to the door. She pulled back the curtain and hissed as the sun blinded her. Apparently she was not just hungover. The tea had also turned her into a vampire.

"Who is it?" Grace called out before hissing again in pain.

"Nabi," came the chuckled response.

Grace blinked in surprise and swung the door open. She jumped back out of the bright sun and hid behind the door as Nabi walked in, carrying a brown paper bag and a huge cup of coffee.

"Coffee!" Grace grabbed the cup like a lifeline and took a deep drink.

"I thought I owed you that much after last night," Nabi said as he set the bag down on the kitchen table. "And breakfast. Biscuits and sausage gravy, my favorite. I hope that's okay with you."

"It's great. But I should apologize. I don't ever drink, but I was so nervous," Grace said as she brushed her hair from her face. Oh gosh, her hair. She looked down at her bare feet and old T-shirt. She put her hand to her head and cursed under her breath. Her hair was sticking up everywhere, and she was pretty sure there was a giant crease mark running along her cheek.

"Actually, I need to apologize. Sit down; there's something I need to tell you," Nabi said as he pulled out a kitchen chair for her.

"This doesn't sound good," Grace murmured as she sat.

Nabi took the seat across from her and looked nervously at her. "I swore I could keep it a secret, but I want us to always be honest with each other. I got you drunk so I could ask about your husband."

"What?"

"I was so worried you could only care for him that I kept topping off your drink so you would tell me if your heart was closed to a new relationship." Nabi grimaced. "I know, I was horrible to do that to you."

Grace was so surprised she just stared at him. He fidgeted like one of her students who was in trouble, and for some reason that made her heart soften. "Why?"

"I have not been a saint over the years, but none of those women were relationship-worthy. The past couple years I have been looking for someone I actually wanted to get to know better . . . someone I wanted to make breakfast for. I have been on so many first dates, but no one has sparked my interest. I was about to send my father a request that he arrange a marriage when I met you. The spark was immediate. But being a widow, I didn't know if your heart was still wed to someone I could never compete with."

Grace shoved her chair back. "I'm so sick of this widow crap! Yes, I had a husband. Yes, I loved him. But that doesn't mean I don't want to be loved again. It doesn't mean I don't dream of marriage, a family, and someone to share my life with. I'm not dead!"

Nabi jumped up and wrapped his arms around her. "I know. I found that out last night. I'm so sorry. I was just so afraid to get my hopes up. And here I go and ruin the chance I was given. Please, Grace . . . please say you will give me another chance. Just one more date."

"I felt it, too, Nabi," Grace whispered against his chest. She took a deep breath. She closed her eyes and heard the steady pounding of his heart. She felt him breathe. She smelled horses and the outdoors. She wanted to be near him forever. "I will give you one more date on the condition that you ask me if you want to know something. I'll always tell you the truth."

Nabi leaned back so he could look in her eyes. "I promise. I'll also always tell you the truth. You'll never regret giving me a second chance." Nabi leaned forward and pressed his lips to hers. Heat flared through her body in response.

"Tonight at six. I'll pick you up for dinner. Then maybe we could go riding afterward."

Grace would have responded, but that kiss had tilted her world more than a whole pitcher of the Rose sisters' special iced tea. Instead, she just nodded and watched as he left. The door closed, and she stared at it for a full minute before breaking out into a little happy dance, accompanied by a squeal of delight and then a moan of agony. Aspirin first, then breakfast.

Nabi smiled the whole way back to the farm. He pulled up to the security building and noticed the bicycle leaning against a tree. He entered the key code and swiped his badge by the steel door. It unlocked, and he walked into the building. Two security guards sat at the computers, monitoring all the cameras on the farm, while other guards patrolled the grounds.

"Morning, boss," they called as he walked in.

"Morning. Anything interesting going on?"

"Nope. Just getting ready for the Prince James of England's visit to look at his new colt. We are coordinating security with Mr. Ashton's farm as well, since the prince will be visiting both locations."

"Good. Let me know when you've completed the protocol, and I'll look it over to finalize it." Nabi looked around the darkened room and saw what he was looking for at the small desk in the corner. He walked over and peeked over her shoulder. "Who is Nolan?"

Abby shrugged and continued to look at Nolan's report card she had managed to find on the school's database.

"What happened to Corey?"

"Corey's a tool."

Nabi reached forward and clicked off the screen.

"Hey! I was looking at that."

"Sometimes it's better to just ask about them instead of investigating and interrogating," Nabi said before giving her a quick pat on the head. "So, who's this Nolan character?"

"He's so nice. He's in my science class. We danced last night, and then he texted me just to make sure I got home all right. Zain and Gabe are driving me to the Blossom Café this afternoon after Nolan gets off work. We're going to get a milkshake together."

"Work? That sounds promising. He's fifteen and works?" Nabi asked impressed.

"He's sixteen, and he works at the feed store during the summer. His parents own it."

"Nolan Flynn? He's a good kid. And your parents allowed this?" Nabi asked, surprised.

"He asked Dad this morning when Dad stopped at the feed store. He was so impressed that a boy actually talked to him. He said he would allow it if someone else was also there. The twins said they would go. They're good friends."

"Yes, they are."

"How did your date go?"

"Good. In fact, I'm taking her out to dinner tonight."

"Well, you better seal the deal soon because my friend Megan saw you go into Mrs. D's house last night and told everyone at the field party. Now everyone knows Mrs. D actually wants to date. The guys are lining up to ask her out. Megan's dad said he was going to ask her out tonight when he got home from work."

Nabi groaned. Of course! He'd finally found someone he was interested in, and half the town was going to go after her. "Megan's dad? Isn't he your father's age?"

"So?"

"Shit," Nabi cursed before storming from the security

77

building. He headed for the barn to do a little manual labor and found Ahmed, Mo, and Will looking over a horse that was getting ready to foal.

"What's gotten you so mad?" Ahmed asked as the three men turned to look at him.

"Was the date last night that bad?" Mo questioned.

"We thought with our advice it would go well," Will sighed. "Sorry, man."

"I messed up and interrogated her," Nabi said through clenched teeth.

The men sucked in a breath and looked at each other. "What technique did you use? Please tell me you didn't use the Reid Technique," Ahmed said slowly.

"No, I used the Rose sisters' special iced tea technique. And then I told her about it this morning. She was reluctant, but she forgave me and gave me one date to prove myself."

"Oh," the men all said, knowing what a powerful technique that really was.

"And now I have found out every other single man in town wants to ask her out since she went on a date with me."

"Then you need to stake your claim," Mo told him.

"Very publicly," Ahmed agreed.

"And there's only one place to do that." Will nodded.

"The Blossom Café," they all said together. Daisy and Violet's restaurant was ground zero for gossip. He had planned to take her to a nice place in Midway or Lexington, but they were right. He had to go big or go home.

"Is she worth taking the relationship to the next level?" Ahmed asked.

Nabi didn't have to think about it. "Yes, she is."

"Then good luck," Will said as he shook Nabi's hand. "You'll need it."

Chapter Ten

G race looked in the mirror and slid the lip gloss across her mouth. The pale pink matched the shirt she was wearing. Nabi hadn't called her to tell her where they were going, so she went for jeans and a pretty top. However, three fathers of former students had called her today. They had all asked her out. She had politely put them off. Tonight would determine if she called them back or not. There was just something about Nabi that made her heart race and her whole body feel happy. She smiled, she laughed, and she wanted to be held in his arms. She didn't feel that way about any of the dads who had called her.

The doorbell rang exactly at six, and she hurried from her bathroom. She opened the door and smiled at Nabi. He looked sinfully handsome in a dark black suit. "Am I underdressed?"

"No, you're perfect. Like always."

"I wasn't perfect this morning," Grace laughed.

"I'd never seen anyone look so beautiful as you did." Nabi stepped forward and placed a soft kiss on her cheek. "Jeans, dresses, naked, in the dark, or first thing in the morning. I'll always find you beautiful."

Grace felt her body tingle in each spot his lips kissed. She felt happy. She felt desired, and she felt beautiful. She couldn't wait to see how this date went.

"Ready for dinner?"

"Yes. Where are we going?"

"To the Blossom Café."

Grace stumbled, but Nabi was there with a steadying hand. "Is that okay with you? I promise I won't order the special tea," he teased.

Was she okay with it? In a small town like Keeneston, going to the café for a date was like a public announcement of a serious commitment. "Are you okay with it?" Grace asked instead of answering.

Nabi nodded and smiled at her. "I am. There's something about you my soul recognizes, and I would like nothing better than to share whatever it is with you."

Grace took a deep breath. "I would like that, too. But, let's see how tonight goes before we make any decision on what happens next. Right now, it's dinner. Then we'll just see what happens."

"Sounds good." Nabi opened the car door for her and waited for her to settle in before closing it. His stomach was in knots, but his heart was full. He'd known the second she'd opened the door to him this morning that she was the one. Now he just needed to prove it to her.

Nabi parked on Main Street. The summer nights were long, and the sun cast a warm glow on the tiny town. Doors to shops were propped open as customers chatted and browsed. The flowers surrounding the café were in full bloom in old bourbon barrels. People sat at bistro tables on the sidewalk and talked as the young waitresses helped take orders and deliver food.

While the Roses didn't want to admit it, they were getting older. They'd hired two waitresses so Daisy could help Violet in the kitchen. Violet wasn't ready to let go of that responsibility. And Nabi was perfectly happy to have her making his favorite foods every day. If only he could get Mo's French cook to match them. Gosh knows, he and Mo had tried.

"Are you sure about this?" Grace's soft voice stopped his hand from reaching for the screen door.

"I am. Are you?" Nabi asked, admittedly a little nervously. He wasn't one for wearing his heart on his sleeve, and in Keeneston, taking a woman to the café was telling the whole town your feelings.

Grace slipped her hand into his. She looked down at their intertwined fingers and smiled. His hand engulfed hers, but he was so gentle and strong at the same time. The feeling gave her comfort. "I am now. Let's do this."

Nabi opened the screen door, fully aware that all conversation had stopped as the patrons waited to see whether he and Grace came in or not. Daisy Mae Rose pushed the young waitress out of the way.

"I got this, dear." Daisy paused in front of them. "Are you joining us for dinner?"

Nabi smiled and gave Grace a reassuring squeeze with his hand. "Yes, table for two, Miss Daisy."

"Dang, we really needed new pew cushions," Father James said as most of the patrons joined him in groaning over their lost bets. He looked into Nabi and Grace's surprised faces and smiled. "May you have a blessed dinner. Tell me, are you thinking of a fall wedding?"

And with that, the bets erupted. Daisy waved the waitress over to take their order since she was too busy taking bets on the potential Nabi/Grace wedding.

"Well, that certainly wasn't what I expected," Grace said as she suspiciously sniffed the iced tea placed in front of her.

"The last I heard, I was the longest outstanding bet. I

think most people had me dating a Belle."

Grace absently looked away. Nabi was starting to recognize that as her signal for getting nervous.

"Thank goodness I found you. The Belles are practically children. I've always wanted a woman who was already secure in herself and didn't need a husband to define her. I would rather be your partner than your social catalyst."

Grace smiled at him then and he felt as if all the betting patrons had simply disappeared. His new mission in life was to make Grace smile. She was so beautiful, and he didn't want to lose her. He already knew . . . she was like a warm blanket wrapped around his heart. Grace was the one. He was going to delete that email as soon as he got home.

"I just want you." Grace flushed bright pink and stuttered. "Not like that—well, yes, like that, too. But I was trying to say I like you for who you are, not for what you can do for me. That's a pretty selfish type of love, isn't it?"

"I couldn't agree with you more—I want you, too. In every way I can get you." Nabi winked and enjoyed seeing the surprise and then desire spark in her eyes.

Grace took a large drink of iced tea and wished it were spiked. How did she respond to something like that? He was so masculine, so sexual. She was, well, she wore cotton panties that came in a six-pack. How could he want her? And then when he got her, would he be disappointed?

However, the idea of a naked Nabi leaning over her to kiss her . . . and then so much more, kind of made her panties irrelevant. Grace took another drink to cool off. Why was it so hot in here?

"So, tell me how you came to Keeneston." She took a deep breath as Nabi told her of his transfer at twenty-one. It didn't help. Her eyes were undressing him, and she couldn't stop them — she didn't want to stop them.

Her head shot up from where she was mentally unbuttoning his pants when his hand covered hers on the table. Nabi leaned forward and dropped his voice. "If you keep staring at me like that, I'm going to have to toss you over my shoulder and make love to you as soon as we find someplace semi-private."

"Promise?" Grace sighed and then shook her head with surprise. "I said that out loud, didn't I?"

Nabi laughed and the roar of betting only increased.

"Did they just bet that I was pregnant?"

Nabi only laughed harder. "This is the best date I've ever been on."

His laughter was contagious. Grace felt her stomach tighten and a giggle race up her throat. It was the first time she'd laughed with a man in . . . well, she couldn't remember when. It was nice. "Sorry, we got sidetracked. You were young and the king sent you here . . ."

Nabi nodded and went back to telling his story, although he left his hand on hers. "I trained with Ahmed. I learned how to be an elite soldier and how to run security for the royal family. My father is ready to retire, and he's asked me if I would like to come back to Rahmi. But Keeneston is my home now."

Grace let out a sigh of relief. "I'm glad, although I am sure Rahmi is beautiful."

"It is. But I'm happy to be here. I have friends and a whole bunch of adopted nieces and nephews."

"Do you want children of your own?"

"Very much," Nabi told her with a longing that had her heart contracting.

"Me, too." Grace cleared her throat. "Do you have to leave the country much?" she asked to change the subject.

They had gotten very personal very quickly.

"Some, yes. Dani and Mo are starting to travel more on behalf of Rahmi. As their head of security, I organize the trip, go with them, and run point for protection."

"Do you like to travel?" Grace asked. The hope she was feeling was starting to drop. If he were gone all the time, he would be just like Bo.

"If I were in love, I would hate to leave her behind. And I wouldn't have to. Mo lets the wives of his higher-level personnel take them along if possible, and I'm the highest level there is. Grace, I'm not Bo. I wouldn't leave you just because I wanted to travel."

"Come on, let's go for a ride. I bet I can beat you around the track." Grace relaxed and fell into teasing Nabi. It wasn't fair of her to compare him to Bo. For the rest of the night, she was just going to enjoy the here and now.

"Wouldn't a winter wedding be beautiful?" Pam Gilbert, the former head of the PTA and current head of the Keeneston Ladies Group, asked as Grace and Nabi walked past them toward the door of the café.

"Pam," her sister Morgan Davies chided, "she can get married whenever she wants." Morgan coughed "September thirtieth" and then pretended she hadn't said anything. When her sister rolled her eyes, Morgan just shrugged. "Miles and I would love to take a month off after Layne leaves for college."

Nabi squeezed Grace's hand, and they walked off as they laughed.

Grace finished brushing Zoe while Nabi did the same with his horse. She couldn't remember the last time she'd had so much fun. They had raced and then taken the horses for a short ride around the farm as they talked.

"Thank you again for coming to my rescue. I feel so much better knowing Zoe is here," Grace said as she put her brush in her tack box. The barn was spotless. Fresh straw covered the large stalls and fresh oats had just been poured. Zoe was thrilled.

"My pleasure. I'll always be here if you need me." Nabi smiled at her as he closed the stable doors. He stepped over to where she was sitting on top of the tack box. His eyes had darkened, and Grace felt her breath accelerate. He was going to kiss her. She opened her legs slightly so he could step between them. Nabi gently brushed a lock of hair from her face and bent down. His lips brushed hers softly at first. She tentatively placed her hands on his waist and opened for him when she felt his tongue run along the seam of her lips.

Soon there was nothing gentle. She raked her nails down his back, and he deepened the kiss. She sighed with contentment when Nabi finally pulled back and looked down at her. This was a man who would never abandon her. If they were separated and she needed him, he would move heaven and earth to get to her.

"How can I be feeling what I am after just a couple days?" Grace whispered as she brushed his dark hair from his forehead.

"I don't know. I have been waiting so long to feel like this that I still can't believe it's real." Nabi looked into her eyes and the feeling behind them took her breath away. "Should we give it a shot then. You and me?"

"I would like that." Grace rested her head against his chest as Nabi held her tight. She smiled as she felt the excitement of the future strum through her body. She had been given a second chance at love, and she was going to cherish every moment.

"Do you have a ball gown?"

Grace looked up in surprise. "Um, no. Ball gowns aren't the normal attire for kindergarten teachers."

Chapter Eleven

"Shhh!" Abby hissed to Kale who was about to burst from where they were hiding outside the barn.

"What did she say?" Zain asked.

"She doesn't have a ball gown," Sienna told him.

"What would she need a ball gown for?" Reagan wondered.

"I bet it's for the charity ball my dad and mom are throwing for the Prince James of England," Gabe guessed.

"How romantic to be asked to a ball," Riley sighed.

"But when is it?" Piper asked.

"Next week," Ariana answered.

"Oh no! You can't get a ball gown in a week!" Sophie said, sounding worried.

"And they're so expensive," Layne muttered.

"But she has to go! She has to be like Cinderella. Uncle Nabi would surely ask her to marry him then," Cassidy said from where Dylan was holding her to peek through the window of the barn.

"Yeah, I don't know how to help with this one," Jackson muttered as Wyatt, Carter, and the rest of the boys nodded.

"But I do," Sydney smiled.

"How?" Greer asked excitedly.

"I *am* a model. I do know designers." Sydney was

already piecing her next moves together.

"Thank goodness. I was afraid we'd have to go shopping," Ryan said with relief.

"Porter, Parker, what are you doing?" Reagan snapped. Her eleven-year-old twin brothers were climbing a tree with Jace right behind them.

"We're spying. We're going to climb onto the roof and look down the skylight since y'all won't move from the one window," Porter complained.

"And just who are you all spying on?" The woman's authoritative voice caused everyone to freeze.

"Mom!" they all gasped at once.

Kenna shook her head. The women had just finished meeting at Dani's to discuss the charity ball when one of the security guards mentioned the commotion at the barn. So Kenna, Dani, Paige, Annie, Katelyn, Morgan, Gemma, Tammy, and Bridget had all decided to find out what their kids were up to. They had come up over the hill and found them all plastered to the side of the barn. Well, except for Parker, Porter, and Jace who were hanging from a tree.

"Spill," Gemma said as she crossed her arms over her chest and narrowed her eyes at her twin daughters.

"Now," Bridget ordered as if commanding one of her police dogs.

Abby stepped forward with her head held high. "It's all my fault. We found out Nabi was going to email his father to arrange a marriage so we decided to help him fall in love instead, and it worked. But now Mrs. Duvall needs a ball gown so he'll propose, and Sydney thinks she can get one in time."

After years of parenting, the mothers didn't react. You could never show shock to your children or they'd rip you apart. Instead, Annie just shook her head. "And how did you find him true love?"

The kids moved apart to let someone step forward. "We helped, too."

"Miss Daisy!" Katelyn said with surprise.

"Miss Violet!" Dani gasped.

"Miss Lily!" Morgan said shaking her head.

"Well, we couldn't let him enter a loveless marriage," Miss Lily said defiantly.

"And how exactly did you settle on Grace Duvall?" Paige asked.

"That was Cassidy. She thought of her sweet kindergarten teacher, and we agreed they'd be perfect together," Miss Violet grinned.

"Cassidy," Tammy shook her head and gave her daughter the similar look she gave her boss, attorney Henry Rooney, when he practiced a cheesy pick-up line on her. "Where did you learn to interfere in people's lives?"

Cassidy linked their hands together and stepped up to stand next to Abby. "Y'all," she said in her sweet innocent voice. "Like when you and Aunt Morgan fixed Summer up with that nice man at Morgan's office. And like that time Aunt Katelyn and Aunt Annie thought the new sheriff's deputy would be perfect for the teacher Aunt Annie knew. And like that time Aunt Gemma . . ."

"Okay," Tammy said with a roll of her eyes. "So, they've hit it off?"

"They sure have. They were kissing and everything." Greer smiled.

Paige groaned. "And you all have been spying on them this whole time? It was done with good intentions, so we're not mad. But no more spying. And no more interfering."

The kids all shuffled their feet and started whining.

"Enough," Dani ordered. "Now go up to the house and

think about how you would like it if we interfered with your lives like that."

The kids grumbled, but faced with nine pairs of "mom eyes" staring at them, they slowly walked away with three Rose sisters following.

As soon as they were out of sight, the mom's looked at each other and smiled. They quietly tiptoed to the barn and peeked in the window.

"I'm sure Dani or Bridget would let you borrow one." Nabi smiled down to the woman in his arms.

"Oh, they're so cute together," Dani whispered excitedly before being shushed.

Grace shook her head. "I couldn't do that. I don't even know them. Besides, they're both a lot taller than I am. I'm sorry, I just don't think I'll be able to go."

"We'll find a way. I promise," Nabi said before leaning down to kiss her frowning lips.

The moms stepped back from the barn and huddled up. "Cassidy did better than we did," Kenna said.

"Yeah, we've been trying for years to find someone for Nabi with no luck," Dani grumbled.

"And we were outdone by a nine-year-old," Bridget said as she shook her head.

Tammy beamed. "I'm so proud!"

"But, you heard her. She won't ask to borrow a dress, and it's clear they both really want to go," Morgan whispered. She had a gleam in her violet eyes as if she were planning a hostile takeover of a company.

"It would be romantic," Gemma said as she thought about a solution.

"Well, my daughter isn't the only one with fashion contacts," Katelyn smiled. Before she was the town veterinarian, she was one of the world's top models.

"We'll need to get her size," Paige told them as images of the jewelry she sold at her boutique, Lucky Charms, ran through her mind.

Annie rubbed her hands together in glee. "Yes! A chance to do a little B and E. It's been a while since I broke into someone's house."

"I'll go with you and keep watch," Bridget added with a smile that showed she was happy to help Annie with some mischief. "Then we'll call Katelyn and give her the measurements."

"Okay. And we'll stay here and call you when they leave the barn. By the way, they were kissing. It may be a while." Morgan grinned.

"I'll go and pretend to lecture the kids and then get them out of here," Kenna offered. She'd use her best courtroom voice. Being the town prosecutor did come in handy sometimes.

"Do we have to? I mean, they did a good job," Dani asked.

Paige nodded. "True. But then they might figure out we've been spying on them. I mean, really, as if we wouldn't look out the window when their dates brought them home."

The women all laughed slyly. Moms always knew what was going on, and it was foolish to think it wasn't because they spied, eavesdropped, and pried. Nothing would get done if they didn't. That's how they stopped their husbands from buying sports cars they didn't need when they turned fifty. Or stopped their daughters from getting tattoos on their eighteenth birthdays. Or causally mentioned a boy they were interested in wasn't as good as they thought.

It was always done in a way that seemed like casual conversation. "Oh honey, can you believe so-and-so got a sports car? It's so pathetic when men can't embrace growing older. In fact, I find you sexier now. You're so dignified." Or, "Daughter, I'm so proud of you for having a good head on your shoulders and not dating someone like Corey. He's so immature and, from what I heard, doesn't respect his girlfriends very well. Some men have good looks, but that doesn't mean they're good men." It worked every time.

"Don't worry, I'll let them off easy." Kenna smiled as she headed for the house. Annie and Bridget grinned mischievously and hurried to Annie's car while the rest of them raced to hide behind one of the horse vans parked nearby.

"We should let them in on the final product, though," Morgan suggested. "After all, they accomplished what we could not."

The women nodded. "Good. And I am going one step further," Katelyn told them. "I think we should let them come to the ball. They're all old enough, and the prince does have three kids of his own, so he won't be surprised to see them."

"I agree," Tammy put in. "We can let them come after the dinner and the younger ones can stay for an hour and then go to my place. I'll get a couple of babysitters, and they'll have a great time."

"Okay. We'll let them suffer for a couple days before we fill them in," Gemma teased.

Chapter Twelve

Abby shuffled her feet in the large ballroom at Dani and Mo's house. Their mothers had all called them and told them to meet there after everyone got off work. Kenna had lectured them about not interfering in other people's lives. Since then, they had all been bummed out. They had made two people happy and now they wouldn't be able to see if Nabi and Grace would end up at the dance together — a dance that was tomorrow night.

"Are we all here?" Tammy asked as she and the other moms walked in.

"Layne," they all grumbled as they waited for the perpetually late Layne.

Morgan just shook her head as the door to the ballroom was thrown open and her daughter rushed in.

"Sorry!" Layne called as she skidded to a stop next to Piper.

"Well, now that we are all here, I thought you should see this," Katelyn said seriously. She reached into a box, pulled out a dress, and smiled.

Abby gasped. It was a beautiful black taffeta ball gown with a deep V-neck held up with decorated spaghetti straps. The V ended with a white sash around the waist. It met in a bow on the back where the train of the bow fell to the floor.

"It's beautiful!" Sydney exclaimed.

"But what is it for?" Sienna asked.

"It's for Grace Duvall." Katelyn smiled. The girls squealed and the boys fist-bumped each other.

"You're going to help us!" Riley said as they hurried forward for a better look at the dress.

"No, we are going to help Grace. While we don't believe you should have interfered, it's undeniable that Nabi has never been as happy as he is now. We all love him and want to see him happy. So, would you like to have one last mission?" Tammy grinned.

"Yes!" Cassidy said jumping up and down.

"Then, you need to get this dress to Grace without her knowing who it is from. We have a note inside telling her it's a gift for the ball from her friends, but we didn't tell her who, and we aren't going to tell her who," Annie explained.

"And one last thing . . ." Dani held up her hand, stopping the chatter. "You are all invited to attend the ball after dinner. Anyone under fifteen will be able to attend for one hour and will then head over to Aunt Tammy's house for the rest of the evening. Everyone else may stay for as long as they like. And before you ask, yes, you can bring a date if you are so inclined."

"Even me?" Abby asked. She held her breath, not wanting to miss her mother's answer.

"Even you. But we get final approval on the date. Come find us, and we'll talk after the dress is delivered," was all Bridget was able to get out before Abby threw her arms around her.

"You're the best!"

"Now, you all have a mission. So get to it." Katelyn handed the box to Wyatt as they all hurried from the room.

"I can't believe Ahmed is letting Abby bring a date,"

Kenna laughed. "How did you manage that?"

"I didn't. It was his idea." Bridget smiled. "I think he liked the young man she's interested in. He's kind of dorky and cute but showed backbone and a massive amount of respect for Abby and us. I think anyone after Corey would appear to be a saint, so Ahmed's happy. He says he's taught her good taste."

The women snickered. "We have such dear husbands," Gemma grinned. "Bless their hearts."

Grace was sad. She was happy, but she was sad. She turned on the shower and stepped in. She had just come back from a barrel race in Corbin where she'd won enough money to move Zoe to another stable. But she didn't want to. She loved going to Desert Sun Farm and seeing Nabi every day.

She'd gone there every day in the late afternoon and practiced with Zoe. Each day when she'd finished, Nabi had been waiting at the fence to walk back with her and help rub down Zoe. They'd eaten dinner together and shared their nights. Ah, their nights were magical. A week. They'd been together only a week, yet it seemed like forever. She didn't know how it was possible. Since she couldn't remember a time she'd been so happy, she'd stopped caring about time and just enjoyed being with Nabi.

Which brought her to the reason she was sad. Today the Prince James of England had arrived, and Nabi was going to be busy for the next three days. Today was the tour of the horse farms and the visit with his colt. Tomorrow was watching the horse train in the early morning, diplomatic meetings for the rest of the day, and then the ball that night. The prince was leaving the following morning. She wished she could go to the ball. That was impossible for someone like her, though. She wouldn't even know what to do at such an event.

She had learned to dance by watching *The Sound of Music* over and over when she was in high school. She thought prom was going to be very different from what it actually had been, much to her disappointment. And now she'd been invited to a ball but couldn't afford a dress, and she was not going to ask Nabi for money. No way. That would be something Bo would do; this relationship was going to be different.

Grace shut off the water and dried her body. She'd just slipped into a pair of yoga pants and decided to watch *The Sound of Music* when the doorbell rang. She quickly brushed her hair and hurried to the door, but no one was there. Great, there was probably a flaming bag of dog poo on her doormat. But when she looked down there was a large white box sitting there instead.

She bent down and picked it up. Looking around, she didn't see anyone, so she opened the box and pulled out the card.

For tomorrow, from all your friends.

Friends? She pulled back the white tissue paper and almost dropped the box. Inside was the most gorgeous dress she'd ever seen. Grace hurried inside and pulled it from the box. She lifted it up and couldn't believe it skimmed the floor. It was the perfect length, and it looked to be just her size. The doorbell rang again, and Grace hurried to lay the dress carefully on the couch before racing to the door to find another smaller box.

She looked around again and didn't see anyone. She smiled and hurried back inside. She opened the box and pulled out the card.

Every Cinderella needs slippers – from your friends

Pushing aside the paper, she pulled out the most glamorous pair of black heels she'd ever seen. There were crystals and sexy straps and, oh my gosh, they fit! Tears started to fill Grace's eyes as she tippy-toe ran in her sexy heels to find her phone.

"Did you do this?"

"Hi, Grace. Do what?" Nabi asked.

"The dress, the shoes?" Grace sniffed. Her heart was racing. Not in a million years did she think she'd ever wear something so elegant.

"I don't mean to sound like a typical guy, but, huh?"

"Someone just knocked at my door. When I answered, I found a large box. Inside was the most beautiful ball gown I've ever seen. It said it's for tomorrow, and it's from my friends. Nabi, I don't have any friends who could buy me a ball gown this expensive. And it just so happens to be exactly my size. It was you, right? And the shoes. Oh my gosh, the shoes! They fit perfectly!"

"As much as I would love to take credit for this, it wasn't me."

"So you are saying I have some fairy godmothers out there who just happened to know I couldn't go to the ball because I didn't have the money for a dress?"

"More likely do-gooders who like to eavesdrop. Did you mention anything around the Rose sisters or John Wolfe?"

"No. But they knew my clothes size, height, shoe size!

How would they know that?"

"Ah, there's our clue. Do-gooders who can break and enter. I only know two of those. Annie Davies and Bridget Mueez. They must have heard us talking about the ball."

"No, they're so nice. They wouldn't break into my house. Besides, the door has always been locked, and nothing was ever out of place. No one has been in my house."

"Nope, they're just that good. And to get a dress and shoes like that, they needed help. Kenna and Katelyn. And where they go, the rest go. I think the whole group of them just made your wish come true. I, for one, couldn't be happier. So, my dear Grace, will you do me the honor of accompanying me to the ball?"

Grace blew out a breath and looked longingly at the dress and shoes. "I shouldn't. This is too much to accept from people I don't even really know. But, yes. I will. I want to go too much to turn down this gift. I'll just have to find a way to thank them."

"Wonderful! I must admit I wasn't looking forward to going without you. I'll send a car for you at eight. There may be some times I have to disappear for work, but it shouldn't be much. Look, I have to go. I can't wait to see you tomorrow."

"Me, too." Grace hung up the phone and with a squeal of delight grabbed the dress to try it on.

The group of kids all grinned as Grace's eyes went big. They were spread out in multiple hiding places ranging from a tree, the hedge row, and the side of the house. As soon as Mrs. D went back inside after Sydney had dropped off the shoes, they had all run to the next block where their cars were parked.

"That was awesome!" Abby clapped.

"Did you see her face? She was so happy." Layne smiled with pleasure.

"Now we need to get our own dates," Sienna said as she looked at Ryan.

"I'm going to ask Ashley," Ryan said coldly before walking away. Everyone paused, but it didn't look like they were going to learn what was going on.

"I have someone I'm going to invite. I'll see you all later," Sienna said with a fake smile before hurrying to her car. "Carter, can you catch a ride home?"

"Sure," Carter called out.

"That's strange. It's normally Ryan chasing Sienna. Am I wrong or did it look like Sienna was hoping Ryan would ask her?" Sophie asked.

"That's what it looked like to me," Piper muttered as they watched Sienna speed off.

"Are you thinking what I'm thinking?" Gabe asked his brother.

"Yep. We're going stag." Zain smiled.

"Why?" Dylan asked for everyone.

"The ambassador's daughters will be there, and they are hot," Gabe said with a wink.

"Well, I'm going to ask Nolan. Can someone drive me back into town?" Abby cut in as the testosterone level started to rise.

"Sure, we will," Wyatt told her.

"Looks like I need to bum a ride, too," Carter called as he followed them to their car.

"Great job, everyone!" Abby called out. She was just as excited as Grace. Tomorrow was her first ball with her first real boyfriend.

Chapter Thirteen

G race took a deep breath as she waited for the car to arrive at Desert Sun Farm. She tried not to fidget with her dress, so she clasped her hands together as they drew closer to the farm. There was a line of traffic heading there for the ball. Some cars were from local philanthropists and some belonged to government officials from all over the world.

When the house came into view, it took her breath away. Lights lit up the long drive lined with trees and uniformed guards. The house was flooded with light from every window and from cameras flashing outside. The cars stopped as one by one they let their passengers out at the front entrance.

Grace took out her red lipstick and applied it one more time. She'd gone to the new beauty salon in town and had her hair done. The girl had managed to pin it up while allowing some of her more springy curls to highlight her face. At least she looked the part even if she didn't fit in with these political types. It didn't matter. All she wanted was one waltz with Nabi. It had never occurred to her to ask if he could dance. He had that confident air about him that made her think he could do just about anything.

Finally, it was her turn. The door opened, cameras flashed, and she stood up. Grace smiled as she walked the line of photographers. Someone must have notified Nabi because when she looked up he stood at the top of the stairs smiling down at her. Grace almost lost her breath. He was so handsome in his tuxedo with his hair slicked back. When he smiled at her, it made her forget about the photographers. He was all that mattered.

Nabi took a deep breath. Grace was here. His guard had notified him when she'd arrived, and he had hurried to meet her. He didn't want her to walk in by herself. He knew she would be nervous, but when he saw her get out of the car, it was he who turned nervous. That dress . . . he really needed to thank Katelyn. It was the sexiest, most elegant thing he'd ever seen. Grace seemed to float toward him. When she looked up at him, his heart tumbled down the stairs to land at her feet. He was truly head over heels in love.

"You're stunning. I've never seen anyone as beautiful as you."

Grace blushed, but her smiled widened. "Thank you. And I've never seen anyone so handsome as you. I feel like I'm in a movie."

Offering her his arm, he felt so proud when she placed her hand in the crook of his elbow and allowed him to lead her into the ballroom. He didn't take his eyes off her as she stared in awe at the packed room with the orchestra playing in the balcony above them.

He led her to the receiving line, unable to take his eyes off her. He loved her in jeans, but seeing her confidently walk down that line of photographers when he knew how nervous she was gave Nabi one more thing to admire about his spunky kindergarten teacher.

"What are we in line for?" Grace whispered.

"To meet Dani and Mo . . . and the prince."

Grace froze. "I'm meeting royalty?"

Nabi chuckled. "You did know they were going to be here, didn't you?"

"Well, yes. But I thought they would be separate from everyone else."

"Dani and Mo don't really do separate. Just give a curtsy and say 'A pleasure to meet you, Your Highness.' It works for all three of them in these situations."

"If you say so," Grace mumbled. Nabi felt her tighten her grip on him. There were only two more couples in front of them when he leaned down and kissed her. Grace's body relaxed into him, and he forgot he was just trying to distract her. She had turned the tables, and now it was he who was distracted.

"You're holding up the line, Nabi, and I sure would like to dance with my wife sometime tonight." Mo's laughter broke the kiss. When Nabi looked up, he realized the couples in front of them were already gone, and in their place stood three smiling royals.

"Some things just can't wait. Allow me to introduce Grace Duvall," Nabi said smoothly.

"A pleasure to meet you, Your Highness," Grace said as she curtsied.

Dani waved off her curtsy and grabbed her hand. "Call me Dani, and this is my husband, Mo."

"The pleasure is all ours, trust me," Mo smiled as he shook her hand. "Your Highness, may I present Grace Duvall, one of Keeneston's esteemed teachers."

Before Grace could curtsey, the prince was shaking her hand. "A pleasure to meet such a beautiful woman." Grace felt Nabi move to her side as the royals all chuckled. "Who is obviously well cared for."

"I am, thank you." Grace smiled as she slipped her hand back onto Nabi's arm. Nabi smiled down at her and led her into the ballroom.

"There's Katelyn and their group. Would you like to meet them?" Nabi asked. The truth was he couldn't wait to show off his good luck to his friends. It was fate that led him to overhear Zain and Gabe and to find Grace. And tonight he couldn't wait to introduce her to everyone he knew.

"I would like that."

The group quieted as soon as they approached. They smiled and shook Grace's hand as he introduced her. The men sent him winks as the women all started talking at once.

"I don't know which of you to thank, or maybe all of you, but thank you for the dress and shoes. Somehow I'll repay you all," Grace told the group of women surrounding her.

"Thank us for what?" Katelyn asked.

"For the dress and shoes. They're more than I could ever have dreamed."

"While they are lovely, you don't have anything to thank us for. We didn't do anything," Tammy said innocently.

Grace giggled. It was too funny.

"What?" Tammy asked.

"It's just that Cassidy wrinkles her nose just like that when she stretches the truth. You can't put anything past a kindergarten teacher."

The women looked at each other and then broke out into laughter. "I think we're going to be fast friends," Kenna said as she gave her a wink.

"I'd like that," Grace said and smiled back.

"And what I would like is to dance," Nabi said as he moved back to her side. "Shall we?"

"I would love to." Grace placed her hand in his as he led her to the dance floor. The other men had moved to lead their wives to the floor, and Grace even saw some of their kids, dressed so beautifully, walk onto the dance floor. The music started and Grace sighed with pleasure as the strands of a waltz reached her ears. Tonight was simply the most beautiful dream come to life. When Nabi started leading her around the floor, she simply hoped the night would never end.

Nolan stood nervously by Abigail's side as her parents took the dance floor. With a tux on, he looked a lot different from the boy in science class. And in her blush-colored ball gown, she felt different than her normal girl-on-the-karate-mats.

"Um, would you like to dance?" Nolan asked with a slight crack to his voice.

"I would love to." Abby smiled as she dragged him onto the dance floor. She stopped next to Nabi and Grace, who were staring into each other's eyes as though the rest of them weren't even there and tried to listen to what they were saying.

Nolan slipped his hand around her waist. When the music started, he led her around the floor with surprisingly smooth twirls. Unfortunately, that meant he led her away from Nabi and Grace.

"You know how to waltz?" Abby asked with surprise.

"My mother made me take dance classes in middle school." He pulled her a little closer, but then her parents danced by and her dad narrowed his eyes. Nolan instantly took a step away from her. If her father kept this up, it would be really hard to sneak away to see what a real kiss would be like.

"Look at Nabi. They look so happy. I wonder what they are saying?" Sophie asked as her date twirled her by Abby and Nolan.

"He said she was the most beautiful woman he'd even seen," Riley told them as she danced past them.

"Nolan, dance us closer," Abby ordered as the rest of the kids seemed to be moving closer and closer to Nabi and Grace.

"That fate had a hand in their meeting," Zain snorted as he danced by.

"And that he had never known he could be this happy," Reagan sighed before being twirled away.

"Grace said she feels the same way," Wyatt said before spinning his date along with the music.

"Nabi then told her he has never felt this way before, but he had been waiting his whole life for this," Layne said with a shine to her eyes.

"For a love to surprise him," Piper said with a smile before being swung away.

"For a love to move him," Carter whispered over his date's shoulder.

"For a love to challenge him to be a better man," Jackson said after dancing away from Nabi and Grace.

"For a love to make him look forward to every new day," Gabe told them as he danced by.

"For a love like this is what dreams are made of." Sydney smiled as she made her way past the couple lost in each other.

"And I love you, Grace Duvall," Abby heard Nabi declare before being whisked away by the dance.

"Grace says she loves him, too," Dylan told them as the

music ended, and they grouped together on the side of the dance floor.

"I think we could all guess that," Sienna said with a smile as they watched the couple kiss as if no one else were in the room.

Abby looked to where Sienna stood with a tall man who had shoulders wider than a door and a body that even sixteen-year-old Abby knew was sinful. But what was interesting was it wasn't him Sienna was looking at with hunger—it was Ryan Parker.

"Oh, isn't it romantic?" Miss Lily sighed as she and her sisters joined the group.

"Another one is going to be happily married, and we couldn't have done it without you kids," Miss Violet said as she clutched her hands to her bosom.

"And now it's time we all celebrate," Miss Daisy said as she looked up to the gentleman at her side. "Let's dance, dear."

"What a wonderful idea," Miss Violet said as she wiped away a tear.

"Then may I have the honor?" The man with the jolly belly and cute accent asked.

"About time," Miss Lily muttered as she watched her sister be led out onto the dance floor.

"What it is, is about time we danced. After all, I lost our bet." John Wolfe smiled down at Miss Lily and held out his arm for her.

"That is true. And I believe there was another part of the bet you still need to fulfill."

John rolled his eyes. "Lily Rae Rose! Not in front of the children."

Abby laughed as John looked tortured saying it, but then he dropped a kiss on Miss Lily's cheek and joined her sisters on the dance floor. She was so glad to see the Rose sisters happy in love. Even though Miss Violet's romance was only blooming, it held great potential, just as she knew it would when she got them together.

"What are you smiling about?" Nolan asked.

"Just thinking about the Rose sisters. I would love to hear their story some day."

"Wouldn't we all," Zain laughed.

"I don't know if we could handle it," Gabe added with a shudder.

"I think they could even make me blush," Ryan joked.

"One day maybe we'll find out," Sydney smiled as they all watched the older couples dance.

"Do you think I'll be a flower girl?" Cassidy asked.

"Honey, I don't think any of the Rose sisters are ready to get married," Piper said as she put her arm around her littler sister.

"No, not them. For Nabi and Grace," Ariana said, pointing to where Nabi was down on one knee out on the terrace overlooking the farm. They were highlighted only by the soft glow of lights. The group held their breath, and when Grace leaped into his arms they knew the answer.

"I think you'll get your wish, Cassidy," Piper smiled.

Abby squeezed Nolan's hand in excitement. Her Uncle Nabi was in love. Her job here was done. "You want to see the library?"

"Didn't your dad say they were locking all the doors?" Nolan asked as they watched Nabi scoop Grace up into his arms and carry her off into the night.

"I wouldn't worry about a little lock if I were you." Abby grinned before grabbing his hand and dragging him down the dark hall.

One hairpin and ten seconds later, Abby opened the

door to the library. After closing the door, the soft sounds of people talking and music playing were still audible. One lamp on the dark mahogany table cast shadows about the room.

She watched as Nolan went to the glass case and looked inside. "Wow, these are first editions!"

"I thought you would like to see them. They're beautiful, aren't they?"

"I didn't think you'd be into literature. You're so . . . sporty."

"So? Does that mean I can't have a softer side? I am a girl, after all. Everyone knows girls have infinite sides and surprises about them."

Nolan smiled at her, and she felt her heart jump with excitement. "A very pretty girl. I still can't believe you'd even give me the time of day."

"I'd give you more than that if you asked," Abby said, suddenly shy.

Nolan stepped toward her and stopped in front of her. "Can I kiss you?"

"Yes," Abby whispered.

She closed her eyes and waited as Nolan's hands cupped her face, and he lowered his lips to hers. This time it was everything she dreamed of and more.

Epilogue

Four months later. . .

N abi took Grace's hands in his. He looked into her eyes and smiled. Today was the happiest day of his life. "I do," he said proudly before kissing his bride.

Their friends and family clapped as husband and wife turned to walk up the aisle. Katelyn had gone dress shopping with Grace. The beautiful gown reminded him of the ball gown she had worn the night he surprised them both by proposing. He hadn't planned it, but he had been bursting with love, and it only seemed natural.

Grace squeezed his hand, and they shared a smile as Ariana and Cassidy threw rose petals into the air. Today his birthday wish had come true. He'd found a woman he loved with the same wild abandon that his friends loved their wives. And if he had anything to say about it, he would be a father in nine months. In fact, he'd even placed a bet at the café on it. It was going to be a great honeymoon.

"I love you, Nabi," Grace said before he leaned down to kiss her outside the reception tent. He couldn't seem to stop doing that today. There would always need to be one more kiss.

"I love you, too," Nabi whispered between kisses.

The sound of a throat clearing made him look up. "Father!"

His dad stood with a small scrawny young man and his mother. His father leaned forward to kiss Grace on both cheeks. "I am so fortunate to have gained such a caring, beautiful daughter."

"Thank you." Grace smiled before being enveloped in her new mother-in-law's hug.

"Nabi, I want you to meet Nash Dagher." Nabi's father introduced the young man at his side. Nabi shook Nash's hand and looked back to his father for further introduction. "Nash has been assigned to learn under you so one day he can take your place, just like you did with Ahmed. That is, if he proves himself."

"It is such an honor to meet you and to train under the great Nabi Ulmalhamash Mosteghanemi. It is my life's dream come true. I just graduated from the military academy with honors. I did my final presentation on you and your use of technology mixed with old-fashioned interrogation techniques to get the most information out of prisoners and informants. The way you uncovered the terrorist plot on the royal family is truly the best intelligence-gathering known to man."

Nabi looked at Nash closer this time. He was maybe five-foot-eight and one hundred thirty pounds, but his bones were large and strong. A smile crept across his face. "Nash, I have just the thing for you to start on while I am on my honeymoon."

"Yes, sir. Anything, sir," the young man sputtered.

"First, help move everything out of my house and to our new home. My bride and I are moving to the former Cross property, now called N & G Farm. Renovations were just completed yesterday. Then move your things into my former house. Second, tell Ahmed I asked him to give you The Workout while I am away. After he has given you instruction, I then want you to go into town and find the Blossom Café. I want you to go into the kitchen and tell the Rose sisters you need to gain weight. By the time I get home, I expect to see you ten pounds heavier and lifting fifteen percent more during your workouts."

"Yes, sir!"

"And when we get back, I expect you to have dinner at our house once a week," Grace said as she slipped her hand around Nabi's arm.

"Yes, ma'am. Anything for Nabi Ulma . . ."

"Just Nabi is fine," he laughed. "Welcome to Keeneston, Nash. And good luck; the military hasn't trained you for anything like this. But now I want to dance with my bride."

Abby watched as Nabi lead Grace to the dance floor for their first dance as husband and wife. She held out her hand, and the group all gave each other high-fives. They had done it.

"Who's the new guy?" Wyatt asked as they turned their attention to Nabi's parents.

"He's from Rahmi. He's here to train under Nabi," Zain told them.

"No way. He's too small to be a soldier. Cassidy is bigger than he is," Piper laughed.

"He has a nice smile, though," Sophie said as she watched him.

"Well, now that our job here is done, who's next on the list?" Gabe asked Abby as the next dance started.

Abby shrugged as she looked away from her friends and to the dance floor. She watched Sienna, Ryan, and Sydney dance by with their dates followed by the Rose sisters. "You never know who's next."

The End

Made in the USA
Lexington, KY
27 June 2016